W9-BRG-399

To the readers
of Silver Bay

William Durbin
6-22-17

Dead Man's Rapids

Other Books by William Durbin
Published by the University of Minnesota Press

Blackwater Ben

The Darkest Evening

Song of Sampo Lake

DEAD MAN'S
RAPIDS

WILLIAM DURBIN and
BARBARA DURBIN

A Blackwater Ben Adventure

UNIVERSITY OF MINNESOTA PRESS
Minneapolis
London

Published by the University of Minnesota Press
111 Third Avenue South, Suite 290
Minneapolis, MN 55401-2520
http://www.upress.umn.edu

ISBN 978-1-5179-0223-0 (hc)
ISBN 978-1-5179-0224-7 (pb)

A Cataloging-in-Publication record for this book is available from the Library of Congress.

Design and production by Mighty Media, Inc.
Interior and text design by Chris Long

Printed in the United States of America on acid-free paper

The University of Minnesota is an equal-opportunity educator and employer.

22 21 20 19 18 17   10 9 8 7 6 5 4 3 2 1

To our grandchildren

Linden, Olive, Abby, and Andrew

May the joy and wonder of learning
be forever with you

Contents

Where the Rivers Run North

April 15, 1899

Blackwater, Minnesota

BEN WARD STOOD on the back deck of the wanigan and looked across the Blackwater River. As far as he could see, huge pine logs were piled high along the west bank. The river had opened up only two days ago, and chunks of ice still clung to the riverbank. Brown, rushing water sparkled in the morning sunshine, but the woods were still patched with snow. The cold air smelled of pinesap, mud, and rotted leaves.

The log drive would start tomorrow morning when the men broke loose the "rollways" and dumped the logs into the river. From the time Ben was a little boy, he had dreamed of joining a drive, and now that he was thirteen he would be working with his pa on the floating cookshack, or wanigan, that followed the log drivers on their one-hundred-mile journey to the Canadian border.

"Your turn," said Nevers, the other assistant cook.

Ben popped a raisin into his mouth and spit it toward the bucket that Nevers had set on the deck. But his shot went long and plunked into the river. "Dang it," Ben said. He knew that log drivers often had raisin-spitting contests, so he and Nevers had been practicing every day.

"Stop fiddling around and sweep this floor," Pa called through the doorway. "The fellas might be stopping by for lunch."

"I swept after breakfast, and it didn't do a lick of good." Ben stepped inside, smelling wood smoke and the hot iron of the cookstove. "The deck on this old boat is nothing but splinters."

"This is a wanigan, not a boat. And I like my kitchen clean." Nevers grinned.

"Something funny, mister?" Pa eyed Nevers.

"No, sir."

"Then make yourself useful." Pa tossed Nevers another broom.

Now it was Ben's turn to smile.

"I'm going up to the store and check on our supply order," Pa said. "After you sweep the floor, you can fill the wood box and polish the lamp globes."

As Pa walked up the muddy riverbank and into the balsam trees, Ben said, "I could do a hundred jobs and never please him. Just once I wish I could work with a cook that wasn't so crabby."

"Careful what you wish for," Nevers said.

"What's that supposed to mean?"

"It's an old saying. Be careful what you wish for 'cause it might come true."

"That don't make sense. Last winter it was hard enough working with Pa at the logging camp. But once the drive starts we'll be stuck on this ramshackle cook boat for six weeks."

"We knowed the quarters would be tight," Nevers said.

"Tight? This boat can't be ten paces long. It's like working on a floating coffin."

Pots and pans hung above the big cast-iron cookstove and the wooden counter that ran along the west wall. The opposite side held a double bunk for the boys, along with shelves and storage cupboards, and a bunk for Pa. A dishing-up table and two flour barrels stood in the middle of the floor. The far corner held several sacks of potatoes and assorted ropes and tools.

"I reckon it'll be tolerable once we get going," Nevers said.

"We've worked three days to get this boat ready, and look at the floor!" Ben took a hard sweep at the splintered planks. "The dirt sticks in all the holes left by the fellas' spiked boots."

"If we lived through fifty-below temperatures last winter with your pa, we can handle one river trip."

"I don't know if I can stand him bossing me all—"

Before Ben could finish, a voice boomed, "Can't nobody get some grub around here?"

Ben turned to see a huge man step onto the deck. The whole wanigan tipped from his weight as he yelled, "Where's that ole reprobate Jack Ward?"

"Jack!" he hollered, ducking his head to get through the doorway. "Your favorite river pig is here!"

Ben stared. He had seen lots of big, strong lumberjacks around Blackwater, but he'd never seen one this big. The man wore a red stocking cap as large as a water bucket. His green plaid shirt was broad enough to make a tablecloth. Like all log drivers', his wool pants were staged, or cut off above the ankles.

The giant man finally turned to Ben. "Who are you?"

"I'm Ben Ward, and this is Nevers."

"Jack's son?" the big man asked.

Ben nodded.

"Well put her there," the man reached out a hand as thick as a ham hock. "I'm Hungry Mike."

Ben watched his hand disappear in Mike's palm, and Mike pumped Ben's arm so hard that his teeth rattled.

Mike looked at Nevers and Ben. "You two brothers?"

"He's just my partner, but he's been staying with us." Ben wondered if Mike was joking about Nevers being his brother, since Ben had blond hair and pale, freckled skin, while Nevers was dark haired and tanned easily.

Mike's lively green eyes scanned the counter. "I see you got some fresh doughnuts. I could do with a morning snack."

"Help yourself," Ben said. "I'll pour you some blackjack." Ben picked up a tin cup and reached for the coffeepot.

"If you don't mind, I take my blackjack in a bowl."

Ben had never heard of drinking coffee from a bowl, but he filled one and handed it to Mike.

"Thank ye kindly." Mike reached for the doughnuts on the cooling rack and speared one with each finger and one with his thumb. Holding up all five, he said, "There ain't nothing in the world that compares to Jack Ward's doughnuts. Unless it's his vinegar pie," he chuckled.

Mike sat on a flour barrel next to the dishing-up table, dipped a doughnut into his coffee, and downed it in two bites. Ben was used to lumberjacks who talked sparingly, but Mike gabbed the whole time he ate.

"Has Jack taught you his cooking tricks?"

"Some," Ben said. "We worked with Pa last winter."

"I'm glad to hear you got a season under your belt. I couldn't bide greenhorns cooking on a drive." Mike polished off another doughnut and slurped down more coffee. "You say your partner here is called Nevers?"

"Pa gave him that name."

"My real name's Nathaniel Evers," Nevers said, "but Mr. Ward cut it down to Nevers."

"That was a good choice on Jack's part. Nathaniel's way too long a name for a little slip of a fella like you."

Nevers straightened up to his full four feet eight inches and puffed out his chest. "I might be short, but I'm tough."

"I don't doubt that you are." Mike reached out and speared five more doughnuts.

"Nevers has been on his own since he was eleven," Ben said.

"That's right," Nevers said. "I run off from an orphans' home in South Carolina. They caught me and brought me back three times. But on my fourth try I made it all the way to Minnesota."

"You are a tough one then," Mike said.

"We'd better fill the wood box, like Pa asked," Ben said.

"You boys go ahead and do your jobs," Mike waved his mitt-sized hand. "I'll help myself to some more blackjack."

Just then a voice spoke from the doorway. "Looks like our drive boss will hire any old bum."

Ben turned. Pa was back.

"Jack Ward! You outlaw!" Mike hollered. Setting down his bowl of coffee, he got up and shook Pa's hand.

"You just get here?" Pa asked.

"I figured it must be close to lunchtime," Mike said.

"Didn't the boys give you some doughnuts?" Pa asked.

"I had a couple. But not enough to spoil my lunch."

Hungry Mike and the Doubleheader

BEFORE BEN COULD TELL PA how many doughnuts Mike had really eaten, Nevers said, "Here comes Mac."

The drive boss, Mac MacDougal, was a no-nonsense fella who had a reputation for moving logs downriver, no matter how tough the conditions. But his nerves were touchy, and he had the gloomy look of a fella who was always waiting for something to go wrong. In Nevers's opinion Mac was a permanent sour-face.

"I see Mike has found his way to the kitchen," Mac said. "No surprise there." Mac was a head shorter than Mike, but his ramrod-straight posture made him seem taller than he was.

"Hey, Mac," Mike said. Then he looked at Ben and Nevers. "You boys listen to Mac. He's the best drive foreman that ever was. If you want to test him, toss a bar of soap into the river and watch him ride the bubbles to shore."

"Hungry Mike has been known to exaggerate," Mac said. "By the way, Mike. I figured that big breakfast you had up at Nell's would hold you 'til lunch."

"If that don't beat all!" Nevers said.

"I had me a doubleheader," Mike admitted.

Pa nodded. "That'd be your usual."

"What's a doubleheader?" Ben asked.

Mike said, "A dozen eggs plus a double order of pancakes and bacon."

Ben and Nevers stared in awe at Mike. They'd fed eighty lumberjacks all winter, but no one had put away that much food.

Mac turned to Pa. "Is the wanigan set to go?"

"Pretty much."

"Nothing missing or busted?"

"Nope," Pa said.

Mac almost looked disappointed by the good news. "Since we're starting in the morning, some of the crew will be dropping by for lunch today."

"I expected they might," Pa said.

"I'm looking forward to that," Mike smiled and rubbed his hands together. "Jack's doughnuts have got me in the mood for some serious eating."

"You're always in the mood," Mac shook his head and walked out the door.

"Let's get cooking," Pa said, lifting the lid on the bean pot that had been simmering since breakfast. "These are ready. We'll do up some biscuits, side pork, and potatoes. You boys peel the spuds. I'll mix the biscuits."

Ben opened a gunnysack of potatoes, while Nevers fetched a pail to hold the peeled ones. And when the boys grabbed paring knives, Mike sat down to watch.

"I can tell you fellas are a good team," Mike said.

Mike sipped his coffee as the boys worked. Soon Mike's eyes wandered to a shelf beside the stove. "Looks like some pies up there," Mike said. "Any chance you got an extra?"

Ben was shocked, but Pa never looked up from his mixing bowl. "Those pies are for lunch, Mike Donnelly. You ain't about to starve in the next hour."

Before the boys finished the potatoes, two more jacks

stopped by. The first man, Slim Cantwell, had been a top loader and a favorite of Ben's at the logging camp last winter. Pa waved at the coffeepot. "Help yourself to some blackjack before Mike guzzles it all down."

"Don't mind if I do," Slim said. As he walked to the stove, he nodded at Ben. "Hey there, Benjamin. You and your partner ready for some white water?"

"Yes, sir," Ben said.

Slim was a silver-haired fella, tall and lean, who wore a gray Stetson and always had a pipe in the corner of his mouth. Soft-spoken and never one to brag, Slim was known as one of the best loggers in the north woods.

Just then another man walked in. When Pa saw that it was Charlie Harrigan, instead of giving him a friendly greeting, he only said, "Charlie."

"Jack," Charlie answered back in the same frosty tone.

Nevers looked at Ben and rolled his eyes.

Pa and Charlie had been bickering since the logging season ended last month. It all began when Charlie started courting Evy Wilson, the widow lady who ran the boardinghouse where Pa and Ben lived. Evy had helped Pa raise Ben after his mother died. Pa had never hinted he was interested in her, but once Charlie showed up with a box of candy, Pa threw his hat into the ring.

For the past month Pa and Charlie had been trying to outdo each other. They'd bought Evy handkerchiefs, which she didn't need, and perfume, which she didn't want. And they tripped over each other trying to see who could carry her groceries home. All the fussing irritated Evy, and it embarrassed Ben. But Pa and Charlie kept carrying on like lovesick schoolboys.

"Got those spuds peeled?" Pa asked Ben.

"Almost," Ben said.

"Once you're done, you can fetch some water. We got plenty

of blackjack, but we need to boil up some swamp water for the boys who don't want coffee."

Mike frowned at the mention of tea. "I never could figure why a fella would drink that stuff."

"I favor coffee myself," Pa said. "But the world's filled with all sorts."

Once the potatoes were in the pot, Ben carried in an armload of wood. Then he grabbed the two ten-gallon milk cans they used for hauling water, while Nevers untied the canoe. A firewood raft and a long rowboat called a bateau were also tied to the deck.

Nevers steadied the canoe as Ben set the water cans and a pail in the middle. "Be careful," Hungry Mike called. "Do you know why a canoe is like a baby?"

Before Ben could say that he'd heard the joke before, Mike said, "A canoe and a baby can both wet you without warning," then he laughed a big belly laugh.

"Don't dawdle now," Pa called.

As the boys paddled upstream, Nevers said, "It's right pretty. Reminds me how I miss the Carolina sunshine."

"The leaves'll be out soon," Ben said, looking at swollen pussy willows along the bank. The scent of partly frozen earth hung in the air.

"Back home it's already planting time," Nevers said.

"Summer comes quick in the north woods, but it ends even quicker," Ben said. "Pa claims the weather in Minnesota is six months of winter followed by six months of rough sledding."

"That sounds about right," Nevers laughed.

The Blackwater was rising from snowmelt, and the current was strong. Though the river was fifty yards across today, Ben knew it would shrink to a trickle by midsummer. Since the water was brown and silty, the boys had to paddle a quarter of a mile above town to a feeder stream.

They passed Main Street, which was muddy and badly rutted. The wooden storefronts facing the river reminded Ben of a Wild West dime novel. Blackwater was famous for having twenty-six saloons and only one, poorly attended church. The other businesses were Nell's Hotel and Restaurant, a general store and post office, a Finnish sauna that offered baths for a dime, and Collins Feed Store, which also served as a livery stable and an undertaker's parlor.

For ten months out of the year Blackwater was a quiet town of two hundred, but in the spring and fall when the lumberjacks passed through, the population swelled to over two thousand. Spring was the rowdiest time. The "rough and ready" jacks roared into town, blew their stakes, and limped home, broke and busted.

"Spring in Carolina means azalea and jasmine blossoms," Nevers said. "But around here there ain't nothing but the stink of blind pig whiskey and cheap cigars."

"There's the roof of Evy's house," Ben pointed.

"You reckon your pa and Charlie aim to quit squabbling once the drive starts?"

"I wouldn't bet on it. Since this nonsense started with Evy, Pa's been as ornery as a polecat."

"Chasing after women drives fellas plumb crazy."

"Promise you'll slap me if I ever go goofy over a gal?"

"I will," Nevers said. "And you do me the same favor."

As they fought the rushing current, Nevers said, "It still don't seem right to be paddling south but heading upstream."

"I told you we're so far north the water flows to Hudson Bay. There's the creek just ahead."

The boys pulled into the clear stream and nosed the canoe onto shore. Ben took the lids off the water cans, while Nevers dipped a pail into the water.

Once the cans were full, Ben turned the canoe to head back. But as the bow swung, Nevers said, "That's strange."

"What?"

He pointed. "Something's floating over yonder."

Ben squinted in the sunshine. All he could see was a spot of green. "Let's take a look."

As they paddled closer, Nevers peered through the over-hanging brush.

"What is it?" Ben asked.

"Oh my Lord!" Nevers shouted, back paddling wildly.

"Careful!"

"Paddle!" Nevers thrashed the water.

Ben was about to yell at Nevers again, when he saw it. Wearing a green plaid shirt and half frozen in the ice, a dead lumber-jack floated face down.

"I said, paddle!" Nevers yelled.

"I am!" Ben joined in, pulling hard.

As they backed away, Ben saw the dead man clearly. His face was turned toward them, and his black hair waved in the current, making him look eerily alive. But the scariest thing was one pale hand that bobbed up and down, as if it were beckon-ing them.

The boys paddled double time back to the wanigan. Nevers kept shaking his head, and despite the sunshine, he shivered.

"You okay?" Ben asked.

But Nevers wouldn't talk.

"You gonna be all right?"

Nevers finally spoke in a trembling voice. "I stared straight into his eye, Ben. Minnows was picking at his lips. I never told nobody this, but my jitters around dead folks started the night my mama died. We'd lost my little sister Charlotte to the flu, when Mama came down with a powerful fever. I sat up with her all night. Toward dawn she seemed better, and I dozed off in the chair. The next thing I knew, I snapped awake with the sun full in my face and me holding her cold hand. I couldn't help but scream. That was the start of my orphanage days."

"I'm sorry," Ben said.

"You got nothing to be sorry for," Nevers said. "At least I can remember the good times I had with my mama. But that's something you got shorted on yourself."

Ben nodded to himself as he pulled on his paddle. Nevers knew that Ben's mother had died when he was just a baby, and his memories of her were as clouded as the one water-stained photograph of her that stood on the dresser at home.

When they pulled up to the wanigan, Hungry Mike stood smiling on the deck. "Looks like that canoe didn't wet you."

"We saw a dead body," Ben said.

"What's that?" Mike frowned like he'd misheard.

"About time you got back," Pa yelled from inside, "we need to get that tea water boiling."

"There's a body froze in the ice, Mike," Ben said. "Across from the creek."

Pa started to holler again, but Mike called, "We got trouble, Jack."

As Mike helped Ben and Nevers climb onto the deck, he said, "You boys did good not tipping your canoe. I'd a jumped outta that little boat myself."

When Pa heard about the dead man, he frowned at Ben. "Didn't I tell you that some of those crooked saloon keepers steal money from the jacks and dump their bodies in the river?"

"Yes, Pa."

"For heaven's sake, Jack," Mike spoke up. "Knowing that fellas get killed is a whole lot different than seeing a dead body firsthand." Mike shook his head. "I'll go up and tell Jim Collins at the funeral parlor."

3

Broke and Busted

PA WALKED INTO THE KITCHEN with the boys trailing behind.

Ben whispered to Nevers, "You sure you're okay?"

Nevers nodded, but he still looked pale and shaky.

After the boys filled the hot water tank beside the stove and started the tea water boiling, Pa said, "We'd better get the nose bags out for tomorrow."

"Are we fixin' to feed horses?" Nevers asked.

"I don't mean a feed bag." Pa pulled a dozen canvas sacks out of the cupboard. "I mean these." He showed Nevers the long strap. "This goes over a fella's shoulder so his lunch can ride out of the way behind him."

"Why are they so big?" Ben asked.

"Remember how I told you we serve four meals on a drive?"

"Breakfast, first lunch, second lunch, and dinner," Ben said.

"That's right. The jam crew and drive crew can't make it back to the wanigan until dinner, so they carry two lunches."

"That's why I favor the sacking crew." Mike was back and standing in the doorway. "The work might be wet and muddy, but it keeps me close to Jack's kitchen."

Two more men showed up. After meeting Hungry Mike, Ben was curious to see what the other log drivers would be like. Pa was fond of saying, "Every log driver is a lumberjack, but not every jack has what it takes to be a log driver."

One of the new men was a skinny fella with a wrinkled face, pale green eyes, and tufts of gray hair sticking out from under his weathered slouch hat. Most river pigs were young, but he looked like a grandpa and walked with an unsteady gait. Ben couldn't imagine him riding logs.

"Jimmy McClure!" Pa shook his hand. "You said you was retiring from log driving."

"Hey there, Jack." Jimmy wore a permanent grin, and he spoke with a raspy voice and a Maine accent that turned his *r*'s to *ah*'s. "I got me a new wife who likes pretty things. So I need to earn some cash money quick." Jimmy winked at Ben and Nevers.

"You old coot," Mike said. "How many wives have you burned through now?"

"I done lost count," Jimmy said.

Mike grinned at Ben. "Jimmy's so skinny it takes him ten minutes to cast a shadow."

"He might be thin," Mac said, "but he can put away the beans with the best of them."

"Tell the boys how they cooked beans back in Maine, Jimmy," Pa said.

Ben was looking forward to hearing Jimmy's recipe, but a deep voice boomed. "What's this? An old loggers reunion?"

A tall, sandy-haired fella stepped inside, and Jimmy said, "I got plenty of miles left on these old legs."

"I don't doubt that you do, Jimmy," the tall man said slowly, his words muffled by a big chaw of tobacco.

"Good to see you, Dynamite Dick," Mike said, as he and Jimmy took turns shaking Dick's hand. Dick matched Mike's height, but he was only half as wide across the middle. Dick's eyes were a pale, mischievous blue, and he was missing one front tooth. His beard, teeth, and once-red shirt were brown with tobacco stains.

Ben saw Nevers wrinkle his nose at Dick's spit-stained shirt. Nevers hated chewing tobacco so much that he'd once told Ben, "I'd rather put a gob of mud in my mouth than chew."

"Why do they call you Dynamite?" Ben asked.

"'Cause of my dynamite personality." Dick's tobacco-stuffed cheeks and his slow drawl made him hard to understand. Especially after listening to Mike talk ninety miles a minute all morning.

"Tell the truth," Jimmy laughed.

Pa said, "Dick's a fine powder man, but he's been known to miscalculate."

Dick leaned back outside and spit a stream of tobacco juice. "That was a long time ago."

"Not that long," Jimmy said. "One spring Dick brought a case of frozen dynamite into the wanigan and set it beside the cookstove to thaw."

With a slow grin, Dick showed his brown-stained teeth. "How was I to know the cook would stoke up a big fire?"

"And how was I to know some sawdust brain would store dynamite in my kitchen?" Pa said.

"You were the cook?" Ben asked.

Pa nodded. "Lucky for me I was on the bank when she blew."

"The whole case went off?" Nevers asked.

Jimmy and Mike both laughed. "It turned that boat to splinters," Mike said.

Jimmy clapped his hands together. "The stovepipe shot up like a sky rocket."

Just then a pale, stringy-haired fella pushed past Jimmy. "Where's the lunch?" the man asked.

Pa's eyes narrowed. "Lunch'll be ready when I say so."

The new fella said, "My name's Klondike. I can saw faster and chop harder than any jack alive." His wrist was wrapped in a stained handkerchief, and his cheek was cut from fighting.

When no one said anything, Klondike sneered at Ben and Nevers. "Why you tadpoles hanging around here?"

"Time to clear out this wanigan," Pa said. "With all of you stomping around, my biscuits are liable to go flat. Find a seat outside. We'll holler when the grub's ready."

The "seats" Pa referred to were a handful of wooden crates and a couple of logs on the riverbank.

After the men left, Pa said, "I'm not used to all that racket in my kitchen."

"Why do they call that fella Klondike?" Ben asked.

"I only met him once. He spouts off about prospecting for gold in Alaska and wears everybody out with his jawing."

Ben knew that Pa hated braggers. True lumberjacks let their work speak for itself like Slim did. The greatest compliment any man could get was simply, "He's a good man in the woods." Slim didn't talk much, but when he did, everybody listened.

When the food was ready, Pa called, "Time to dish up."

With Mike in the lead, all fifteen men lined up to have their plates filled. They jabbered the whole time, which surprised Ben. Last winter in the cookshack Pa had had a "no table talk" policy.

One by one the jacks grabbed a tin plate, and Ben and Nevers spooned up the spuds, beans, and side pork. Pa set out a big pile of biscuits at the end of the dishing-up table, and the fellas took as many as they wanted. Then they walked out the front door and across the second gangplank to the riverbank.

Once the jacks sat down, everyone got quiet except for Hungry Mike, who talked the whole time he ate. He held up a biscuit. "I swear these little beauties are works of art."

"What would you know about art?" Mac asked.

"I know light and fluffy when I see it," Mike went on. "And nobody nowhere can match Jack Ward's biscuits." Mike followed another one-bite biscuit with a spoonful of beans.

"Jack's biscuits keep Mike as happy as a clam at high tide," Jimmy said. "And these are some wicked good beans."

"That's why I hire Jack for all my drives," Mac said. "Good cooking pulls in a good crew."

Hungry Mike kept frowning at his spoon.

"Something wrong?" Mac asked.

"I was thinking it'd be nice if they made these spoons a little bigger."

Nevers, who was lugging the coffeepot up the bank, said, "A bigger spoon! Don't you know you took the serving spoon?"

The fellas all laughed.

After the men had seconds, Ben and Nevers carried out four of Pa's vinegar pies.

"So how many drives have we done, Jack?" Mac asked, as Pa cut the pies.

"By my count we've run this river a baker's dozen."

After Mac polished off his second piece of pie, he stood up, loosened his belt a notch, and began a speech: "At daybreak we're gonna give her tar paper, boys. With Jack's fine cooking to fuel us, we'll have these logs to Canada in record—"

"Where's Charlie Harrigan?" Pa suddenly asked.

The fellas had been so busy eating that no one had noticed Charlie was missing.

"Anybody seen Charlie?" Mac asked.

Everyone shrugged except Klondike, who said, "He told me he was heading to Wilson's Boardinghouse for some chocolate cake."

"Chocolate cake!" Pa spit out the words as if they were poison.

"I wouldn't think nothing of it," Mac said. He gave Klondike a dark look and mumbled, "Some folks are always running off their mouths."

"Chocolate cake!" Pa repeated the words twice as loud and

twice as mean. "I'll show that no-good Britisher what he can do with his cake. No way am I gonna let Charlie Harrigan get between me and my Evy."

"Take it easy, Jack," Mac said.

"I quit." Pa balled up his apron and threw it down.

"Now Jack, don't get all bent out of shape."

"I said, I quit." And Pa marched up the riverbank.

Ben stared. Pa had never quit anything his whole life.

The whole crew was dumbstruck. They all knew Pa was a steady fella and the best cook around.

Hungry Mike looked at Klondike. "Now see what you gone and done." Mike looked sadly at his empty plate. "That'll be the last of Jack's pie for us."

"Don't nobody worry," Mac said. "I expect Jack was just blowing off steam. I'll go up to the boardinghouse and talk some sense into him. It'll be okay. It will."

After Mac left, the men sat in stony silence. The truth was Mac had looked less confident than he'd sounded. And Ben could understand the crew's worries. Good cooks were hard to come by, and everyone had signed on knowing Pa was running the kitchen.

Despite the afternoon sunshine that was smiling on the riverbank and despite the fact that their bellies were full, the men suddenly looked like they were getting ready for a funeral instead of a log drive.

Too Late for the Man Catcher

ONE BY ONE the men set down their dishes and walked up to town. Mike was the last to leave. He patted Ben on the shoulder like he was about to say something, but he just shook his head and wandered off.

Ben knelt down and picked Pa's apron off the ground.

Nevers said, "I'm bumfuzzled that your pa quit."

"Me too," Ben stared at the apron. "Pa always sticks with a job. It don't matter whether he's grubbing out a stump or laying a lattice crust on an apple pie, he finishes things up."

"I warned you about wishing," Nevers said.

"Any man that Mac hires has got to be less crabby than Pa."

"Maybe your pa'll come back."

"Once he makes up his mind, it's set in stone. But after we finish the dishes, I'll go up and check on him."

"That's a good idea. Women can muddle up a fella's brain so bad they ain't themselves."

"If this whole mess wasn't so sad, it'd almost be funny to watch Pa and Charlie carrying on."

Nevers smiled. "You don't often see two old codgers courting the same gray-haired lady."

"Don't forget to knock some sense into me if I ever get addlepated over some girl," Ben said.

"And you crack me upside my head if I slip up."

"Before we do the dishes, let's practice with the raisins some more," Ben said. "Last winter at the camp we didn't stand a chance when the jacks were throwing axes and lifting anvils, but we should be able to hold our own in a raisin-spitting contest."

Ben tried pressing his lips together to build up more pressure before he spit, and he tried funneling his tongue to help aim the raisins. But it took a dozen shots before he and Nevers got one in the bucket.

"A target that big should be a cinch to hit," Nevers said.

"There must be some trick to it we aren't getting."

"But I gotta admit my heart ain't in wasting good food." Nevers looked at the raisins in his hand. "Plenty of nights back home I went to bed with less than this in my belly."

"I don't know if I could stand going to bed hungry."

"It ain't a matter of choice," Nevers said.

Just then a voice called, "You boys still here? I hope you haven't gone and quit on me too." And Mac came down the path.

"Did Pa change his mind?" Ben asked.

"There was no talking him out of it."

"I figured that," Ben said.

"I just wanted to let you know about supper."

"You aim to have us to cook?" Nevers sounded scared.

"No," Mac said. "I wouldn't put that on you."

Ben was relieved.

"I stopped by Nell's and set up a tab for anybody who wants dinner tonight and breakfast tomorrow. I just hope those river pigs don't hit the saloons too hard tonight."

"What are you gonna do for a cook?" Ben asked.

"I didn't have time to go through the man catcher in Duluth. So I sent a wagon to fetch a cook that's been working as a summer watchman down in Camp 14. He'll be here by morning."

The wanigan suddenly tipped again, and a voice asked, "Mac? You here, Mac?"

Hungry Mike ducked his giant head and stepped inside. "We got a big problem, Mac."

"What's wrong now?"

"It's that tab you set up at Nell's," Mike fidgeted with his fingers.

"What about it?"

"Nell told me the tab is good for two bits a meal, but I looked at the menu twice, and I can't find nothing that'll fill me up for a quarter."

"Go ahead and tell her I'll cover you for four bits."

"Thanks," Mike said, a smile returning to his face.

"But keep it quiet," Mac said. "I don't want all the boys doubling down on me."

After Mike left, Mac shook his head and said, "Let's hope Hungry Mike's tab is the biggest trouble we have on this drive."

5

Up in Smoke

ONCE THE DISHES WERE DONE, Ben said, "I'd better go up and check on Pa."

"You want some company?"

"I'd best do it alone. If you're okay?" Ben was worried that Nevers might still be thinking about the dead man.

"Just get back before dark."

When Ben returned only a few minutes later, Nevers asked, "Wasn't your pa home?"

"I came around the corner, and all three of them were sitting on the front porch. Evy was in the middle, knitting like usual and smiling, but Pa and Charlie were staring at their boots like a pair of pouty two-year-olds."

"Sounds like they ain't loosened up none."

"I started to sneak away, but Evy called, 'Benjamin!' She was sweet, and it woulda been fun visiting, except Pa and Charlie kept glaring sideways at each other. I said I needed to help you with some chores and left. Evy even offered me chocolate cake."

"And you turned it down?"

Ben nodded. As good a cook as Pa was, Evy was even better. Her specialty was chocolate cake. It was one recipe she'd never share, claiming the secret ingredient was "a pinch of love."

"There's no way your pa is changing his mind?"

"Not unless Evy marries Charlie between now and breakfast and sends Pa packing."

Nevers chuckled. "What are we gonna do about supper?"

"We got leftover biscuits and beans. And a few doughnuts."

"That suits me."

After the boys finished their beans, Ben put a doughnut on his thumb. "What do you say we have a doughnut-eating contest Hungry Mike style?"

Nevers smiled as Ben slid a second doughnut onto his forefinger. "That's all you're fitting on your puny hand."

"Mike's fingers must be as fat as axe handles," Ben said.

"We only got a few doughnuts left anyway."

"Put two on your hand, and let's see who can down 'em the fastest," Ben said.

Nevers picked up the doughnuts, and Ben said, "Ready. Set. Go!"

Ben took one bite out of the doughnut on his thumb, but it broke in two and fell to the floor.

"I win," Nevers laughed.

"You didn't even take a bite!"

"Are you eating that one?" Nevers looked at the floor.

"We'll make a fresh batch tomorrow and have a rematch."

After the boys got ready for bed, they flipped a coin to see who got the top bunk, and Ben won.

Ben hung his pants on a nail and climbed into bed, but sleep didn't come easily. He kept thinking about Pa. And along with the sound of the current that gurgled and swirled past the hull of the wanigan, the tinny notes of a player piano drifted down from a saloon.

It didn't help that Nevers asked, "What's that?" every time an animal rustled in the dark or a fish splashed.

Ben slept fitfully, dreaming that he and Nevers were paddling up a moonlit river. The shore was lost in shadow, but a big moon shone into the water, lighting up the weeds and tiny, silver minnows. Suddenly, a dead man's face floated into view. Ben jerked back, spilling him and Nevers into the river. And just as Ben surfaced, fighting for air, the fingers of the dead man touched his cheek.

Waking with a start, Ben rubbed his face, trying to wipe away the memory of the cold hand. He wondered if Nevers could hear his heart pounding.

Ben felt like he had just fallen back asleep, when a laughing call echoed across the water. He smiled at the haunting music. Each year the loons arrived as soon as the ice left. The loon laughed again. When the call faded, Ben lay for a moment. The town above was perfectly still.

"You awake?" Ben whispered.

"Course I'm awake," Nevers startled Ben. "After being rousted out all winter by your pa yelling, 'Daylight in the swamp,' I can't never sleep in."

"Me neither," Ben said, climbing out of bed and slipping on his pants and boots. Ben smelled cold ashes in the woodstove as he slid the back door open. A handful of stars still shone in the sky. The deck and the tree branches sparkled with frost.

"Chilly out?" Nevers asked, lighting the lantern that hung from the ceiling.

"Freezing," Ben said, sliding the door shut.

"I'm glad we don't have to feed those jacks by ourselves."

"We coulda handled it." Ben lifted the stove lid, and after stuffing birch bark and kindling into the firebox, he struck a match. The pine slivers crackled and popped, and smoke puffed up before he set the stove lid back.

Ben looked at the empty bunk in the corner. "I almost miss Pa hollering, 'Roll up or roll out.'"

"You're the one who wished for another cook."

"I guarantee the new fella will be an improvement."

"You hear that?" Nevers asked.

"What?"

"A crunching sound, like—there it is beside the stove," he whispered. "A mouse." He reached for the broom. "I'll smash him."

"Don't," Ben said. "That's not a house mouse. Look at his big feet. It's a meadow mouse. Give me that crust of bread."

"You're crazy," Nevers said, handing him the bread.

"Just watch." Ben broke off a piece and pushed it toward the mouse. Barely three inches long, the mouse had a light-brown streak down his back. His tail was as long as his body, and his rear feet were oversized.

The mouse wiggled his nose and hopped forward.

"I never seen one jump like that," Nevers said.

"Some folks call 'em kangaroo mice." The mouse picked up the bread in his front paws and nibbled it.

"He's like a furry little man with giant ears." Nevers laughed too loud, and the mouse jumped two feet straight up.

"Yikes!" Nevers said, scaring the mouse so badly that he dove under the stove.

"That's all right. He'll come out if we leave some bread."

"So what's for breakfast?" Nevers asked, adding two more sticks of wood to the crackling hot fire.

"We've got leftover biscuits. And we need to fry bacon to make sandwiches for the nose bags Pa showed us."

"And we can put some of your pa's oatmeal cookies in those lunch sacks, too."

"We'll have to make a fresh pot of beans. No matter who the new cook is the fellas will want their beans. And we can batch up those doughnuts we talked about."

While the boys simmered the beans and made a fresh pot of coffee, the meadow mouse crept out for a snack. Then he hopped behind the wood box and took a nap.

"He's a cute little critter," Nevers said, stirring the beans. "I'm glad I didn't swat him."

"You realize this is the first morning we ever ate without Pa?"

"I still can't get over him quitting," Nevers said.

"But I know one good thing that's come out of Pa and Charlie's fussing."

"What's that?"

"They gave us a perfect lesson in how not to act," Ben laughed.

"True."

After practicing their raisin spitting for a while, and not improving, Ben said, "Since nobody's here yet, let's make those doughnuts and surprise Mike."

"It'll be a hoot to see how many he eats."

The boys agreed on the amount of flour and sugar, but they couldn't decide how much cinnamon and nutmeg to use. They finally settled on a teaspoon of each.

While the batter rose, Ben chunked more wood into the stove, set the cast-iron skillet on top, and scooped in some lard. "These are gonna be so good."

"The batter looks just right."

"I wonder where Pa put the doughnut cutter?" Ben asked, walking to the cupboard.

"I'll help you look."

When Ben glanced back at the stove, black smoke was billowing out of the pan. "Yikes!" he yelled. Running to the stove, he reached to slide the pan off the heat. But he bumped the coffeepot, spilling coffee into the hot grease.

Flames shot straight up, and grease spattered everywhere.

"Lordy! Lordy!" Nevers yelled.

The boys jumped back to keep from getting burned, as the flames flashed all the way to the rafters.

Nevers picked up a water bucket, but Ben shouted, "Not on grease!"

"Whadda we do?"

Ben shoved a broom handle through the ring of the frying pan lid. Then, leaning as close to the flames as he dared, he dropped the lid with a clank, and it snuffed out the fire.

As smoke drifted out the doorway, Nevers used a towel to smother the last spatters of grease that burned on the stove top.

"Whew!" Ben breathed, his legs shaking.

"I thought we were gonna burn up the whole boat." Nevers's voice was shaky, and his eyebrows were singed.

They dumped out the burnt grease, cleaned the stove top, and scrubbed the floor with soapy water. Then Ben stood on a sugar keg to wash the blackened ceiling.

But even after they'd soaped up everything twice, a burnt smell lingered. Nevers sniffed. "You reckon it's better now?"

"Maybe it'd help if we waved towels by the doors."

Just as Ben and Nevers started flapping their white dish towels by the front and back doors, a voice asked, "What you boys doing? Surrendering? We haven't even started the trip yet."

Ben turned. It was Mike.

"We were just airing the place out," Ben said.

"That's a good idea," Mike said. "It smells mighty smoky in here."

6

Old Sard

"Nevers!" Ben hollered from behind a pine tree where he'd squatted to go to the bathroom. "Bring me some paper. I forgot."

"I'll get it," Nevers called from the deck of the wanigan.

Ben waited, wondering what was holding Nevers up. It should take only a second to tear a page out of the Sears and Roebuck catalog that they used for toilet paper.

When Ben finally heard Nevers coming up the bank, he said, "About time you got here."

"Catch," Nevers said, reaching around the tree and tossing something toward Ben.

"What's this?" Ben asked, as scrap of burlap cut from the top of a potato sack dropped at his feet.

"It was Mike's idea," Nevers called, running down the hill.

"I'll get you for this!"

When Ben got back to the wanigan, Mike was grinning. "Next time nature calls you'll remember your paperwork."

Ben turned to Nevers. "I owe you one."

Just then Mike looked up the bank. "Here comes Jimmy and Dick. Let's get ready to roll some logs."

By ten o'clock the jacks had all gathered on the riverbank. Other than Klondike, who had a black eye to complement his cut cheek and smelled of stale beer, the men looked like they hadn't overcelebrated.

"Did our tadpoles get lonesome last night?" Klondike teased. But none of the fellas joined in.

"'Tis a fine day for driving logs," Jimmy said, admiring the blue sky. "Any word on the new cook yet?"

"Mac told us he'd be getting in this morning," Ben said.

Mike said, "I've got my fingers crossed that Jack will change his mind."

Ben didn't have the heart to tell Hungry Mike there was no chance that Pa was coming back.

Mike pointed at two leftover biscuits on the dishing-up table. "Are those spoken for?"

"They're from yesterday," Nevers said.

"I'll take 'em off your hands."

"I can't believe you got any room after that breakfast you ate up at Nell's," Jimmy said.

"Did he have another doubleheader?" Ben asked.

"I need to keep my energy up." Mike popped a biscuit into his mouth and chewed thoughtfully. "These ain't half bad. Did I ever tell you fellas about the old logger I knew from Hayward, Wisconsin, who put a pinch of gunpowder in his biscuit mix?"

Before anyone could answer, Slim took out his pipe and pointed up the hill. "That might be our new cook coming now."

Ben turned. At the top of the bank a short, round man was walking beside Mac. The fella had a gunnysack slung over his shoulder, and he walked with a limp.

"It's Old Sard," Jimmy said. He pronounced *Sard* as *Sahd*.

"No," Hungry Mike shook his head. "Mac wouldn't never do that to us."

"You know any other cook who wears an eye patch and has a gimpy knee?" Jimmy asked.

"No doubt about it," Slim said. "That's One Pot Pete Sard-man in the flesh."

"Old Sard," Mike sighed. "There'll be no more of these." He stared at the biscuit in his hand. "And we'll be saying good-bye to Jack's pies. Did I ever tell you fellas about Jack's pies?"

"A thousand times," Jimmy said.

But Mike went on anyway. "The crust is so light and crumbly it's pure poetry."

"Since when do you know the difference between a poem and a packsack?" Dick drawled, spitting a stream of tobacco juice, which splattered over his boot.

"Sard's cooking ain't the end of the world," Jimmy said.

"Speak for yourself," Mike said.

As Mac and Sard made their way down the bank, Ben studied the cook. He was bald-headed and had a bushy red beard. A greasy apron covered his round belly, and he dragged his right leg slightly. A black leather eye patch covered his left eye.

Nevers leaned toward Ben and whispered, "He looks more like a fat pirate than a cook."

"Don't make me laugh," Ben said. He didn't want to start off on the wrong foot with his new boss.

"Morning, boys," Mac said. "This here is Pete Sardman. Some of you know Sard already." There were no handshakes or hellos, which Ben took for a bad sign. "I appreciate him stepping in on such short notice."

Though the other jacks weren't as sad eyed as Hungry Mike, no one was happy. River pigs never signed on for a drive without knowing who the cook was. And if Mac wasn't such a well-respected boss, he would've had a mutiny on his hands.

Mac went on. "You boys know the routine. Mike here will foreman the sacking crew; Slim, the drive crew; and Dynamite Dick, the jam crew. We've got a good head of water, so let's lard up and give her tar paper. It's time to push these logs."

Dick walked into the wanigan, grabbed a lard pail, and set it on the back deck. The fellas all took off their boots and socks and scooped out a handful of pig fat to coat their feet and legs.

Two men even peeled off their woolen underwear and stood stark naked, while they rubbed lard up to their waists.

Dick grinned at Ben. "I can tell you thought lard was just for cooking. But it's the only way to stay warm in this icy water." Ben had never heard anyone talk as slow as Dick did. It was like he was leafing through a dictionary to pick out every word.

But the thing that shocked Ben most was Mike's right foot, which was missing his two littlest toes.

"What you staring at?" Mike asked.

"Sorry," Ben said, looking away from the scarred stubs.

"Oh those?" Mike laughed. "I had a little accident back in the winter of '88. Dropped a tree on my foot and crushed it pretty good. Our camp was a long way from the nearest doctor, so when my toes got gangrene, I had to take a hatchet to 'em. Then I shoved the stumps into a fire to cauterize 'em. They've been good ever since."

Ben shivered as he imagined the searing pain Mike must have endured, but Mike only laughed again.

Once everyone was larded up and had their boots back on, Jimmy stepped inside the wanigan. "Choose your weapons, gentlemen," he said, sliding the sixteen-foot-long pike poles off the rafters and passing them outside. The pike poles had sharp steel points on the end and a hook sticking down.

"Those are mean-looking spears," Nevers said.

"They work for both pushing and pulling logs," Jimmy said. "And they're wicked fine for keeping cookees in line." He grinned as he poked at Nevers, making him suck in his belly.

Ben was amazed at how Jimmy kept smiling and joking as he worked—the exact opposite of Mac.

Dick climbed into the bateau and rowed one bunch of fellas across the river. He came back twice more for the rest of the men, spreading them out between the log piles that stretched for a quarter of a mile down the river.

"Are they all gonna work on that side?" Nevers asked.

"Just 'til they bust the logs loose," Ben said.

Nevers looked at the crowd that had gathered on top of the bank. "It's like there's a circus in town."

"The start of a log drive in Blackwater is bigger than Christmas and the Fourth of July all rolled in to one."

"That's 'cause nothing ever happens here," Nevers said.

"Just wait 'til you hear those logs churning."

"Sard," Mac said, as he walked up to Ben and Nevers. "Let me introduce your cookees."

"Vat's that?" Sard said. "Talk to my good side. My right ear's deaf." Most jacks carried their possessions in a flour sack called a turkey, but Sard kept his in a dirty gunnysack.

"I said these are your cookees." Mac raised his voice and pointed at the boys.

"Cookees?" Sard repeated.

"Your assistant cooks."

"I know vat a cookee is. Do you think I'm a dummkopf? I generally cook solo. It don't take a committee to fill up a river pig's belly."

"The boys are good helpers," Mac said. "This is Ben—he's Jack Ward's son—and this is Nevers."

"Ben, eh?" Sard looked him up and down. "How old are you?"

"Thirteen."

"You look weak jawed for thirteen."

"And how about you?" Sard turned to Nevers.

"I'm twelve."

"No, vat's your name?"

"Nevers."

"Vat kind of fool name is that?" Sard said. "I'd say you're more of a snicklefritz."

Sard turned to Mac. "I can't be blabbing all morning. I got to check on those supplies we talked about."

Sard walked into the wanigan and sniffed the air. "Have you dunderheads been playing with matches?"

Without waiting for an answer, Sard walked to the bunk in the far corner. "Looks like this one ain't taken." He tossed his gunnysack under the bunk with a loud metal clank. Then without another word he headed up to the store.

Mac shrugged his shoulders. "He was the best I could do on short notice."

Ben touched his jaw and turned to Nevers. "What did he mean by saying I'm weak jawed?"

"You happy you wished for a new cook now?" Nevers asked.

"Mind your own business, Snicklefritz."

The Long Good-Bye

"BENJAMIN!" The voice sounded far away.

Ben glanced up. Evy and Pa were walking down the hill.

"And look," Nevers said, "Charlie's standing up the bank under those trees." Both boys waved.

"He's not about to let Pa out of his sight."

Evy held her arms out to Ben. "You didn't think I'd let you go without saying good-bye?" She gave Ben a big hug and kissed him on top of the head. Then she turned to Nevers. "And you come here, too," she said, squeezing him tight and tousling his hair.

After hanging back, Pa finally spoke. "I was looking forward to cooking with you boys, but being that—"

"I know how it is," Ben said, trying to put Pa at ease. The truth was he wanted to tell Pa to act his age, but he could see Pa was feeling bad already.

"What you got there?" Ben looked at the sack in Pa's hand.

Pa grinned. "I figured you might have a use for these." He reached into the sack and handed Ben a brand new pair of boots.

"Calks!" Ben said, admiring the shiny black leather and the needle-sharp spikes.

"I got you a pair, too," Pa said to Nevers.

"No fooling?" Nevers's eyes lit up.

"I hope they're the right size," Pa said.

The boys sat on the deck and laced their boots. "Real calks!" Nevers jumped up. "I ain't never had new boots before."

"Do they fit?" Pa asked.

"Perfect," Nevers said.

The boys marched across the deck, grinning as their spikes bit into the weathered planking.

"You better not punch too many holes in your boat," Pa chuckled. "It's got to float you all the way to Canada."

"This is a wanigan, not a boat," Ben grinned.

"So it is," Pa said.

Suddenly a cheer went up from the top of the bank. Ben looked downstream. The river pigs had broken loose the first rollway. A high pile of logs thundered down the bank, crunching and banging into each other. When they hit the river, water splashed all the way to the far bank.

"It's an avalanche!" Nevers said.

The logs kept spinning after they hit the water, and the rough bark made a grinding sound as the logs bumped against each other. The scent of pine pitch was strong in the cold air.

"They'd chew you to pieces if you fell in," Ben said.

Evy moved in for a second round of hugs and squeezed Ben tight. "Are you sure you're ready for this?" she asked. "It seems like only yesterday I was holding you in my rocking chair. I don't like the idea of you going down this freezing river, but I know how stubborn you menfolk are." She looked at Pa.

"Don't forget you've got an important job ahead," Pa said. "Just like an army marches on its stomach, a drive crew needs good food to keep the logs moving."

"We'll do our best, Pa."

Just then gray-haired Jimmy McClure jumped off the far bank and onto a log. Holding his pike pole across his body and grinning, he danced from one log to the next until he made it all the way across the river.

A cheer went up from the townspeople, and Jimmy doffed his hat and bowed.

"Jimmy's the oldest lumberjack I ever met," Ben said. "But he's the happiest."

"And he moves right quick!" Nevers said.

"He must be a good swimmer to risk running across the river like that," Ben said.

"Jimmy can't swim a stroke," Pa said.

"What?" Ben's eyes got big.

"It's true," Pa nodded. "Jimmy claims if he ever goes under he'll just bottom walk his way to shore."

But as quick as Jimmy was, it was clear to Ben that Slim was the steadiest man of all. As the river pigs broke loose one rollway after another, Slim walked the logs with his pipe set in the corner of his mouth as if he were taking a Sunday stroll. And when he stepped from one log to the next, he'd flick the toe of his calk and make the log spin up a rooster tail of water.

"Would you look at that Slim!" Nevers said.

"He's the best there is," Ben nodded. "One time when I was in Sunday school, the teacher asked, 'Who's the most famous person in the history of the world?' He expected Jesus to be the answer, but a little boy shouted, 'That'd be Slim Cantwell.'"

"Hurry, you nincompoop!" a voice suddenly snarled. "Can't you see we got a log drive starting?"

Ben turned. Sard was yelling at a boy who was pushing a loaded wheelbarrow down the hill.

"We'd better get out of your way," Pa said.

Evy patted Nevers on the arm and gave Ben a final hug. "You be careful on that river, Benjamin Ward."

"I will," Ben said. Then he whispered, "And you look out for Pa."

Evy smiled and gave Ben a peck on the cheek. Then she and Pa started up the bank.

Ben had always wanted to be shed of Pa and all his rules, but now that it was actually happening, he suddenly felt alone and afraid.

"What do you suppose that boy's hauling?" Nevers asked.

"Whatever it is, it's wrapped in paper," Ben said, gagging at the smell when the wheelbarrow stopped next to him.

"And it stinks bad enough to knock a buzzard off a gut wagon," Nevers said.

"Don't just stand there gaping," Sard hollered at Ben and Nevers. "Help unload."

Ben looked at a grease-stained package that smelled like smoky garlic. "Sausage?" he asked.

"Talk to my good side," Sard pointed to his left ear.

"I asked if it's sausage?"

"Ja, sausage," Sard smiled proudly. "And Wiener schnitzel." He turned and tossed a package to Nevers. "Lug 'em inside."

When Nevers stepped forward to help, Sard spun around. "Don't be sneaking up on my blind side, you numskull!"

As they carried the packages inside, Nevers whispered, "You still glad you wished for a new cook? You can't talk to his right side, and you can't walk up to his left."

"We'll get used to him," Ben said.

After the boys unloaded the wheelbarrow, Sard said, "Now hang 'em from the ceiling."

"Y'all want the whole lot strung up?" Nevers asked.

"Vat's a yawl? Talk American," Sard snapped.

After Ben and Nevers had the sausages hung from the rafters, Sard smiled for the first time. "Now we got real food."

Ben coughed at the greasy, garlic stench, and Nevers couldn't stop rubbing his eyes. Thanks to Sard, from now on the wanigan was going to smell like the inside of a butcher shop.

Ben heard a rumble and a splash as another pile of logs rolled into the river. The men were working their way back upstream with each rollway they broke loose.

But this time instead of a cheer from the crowd, Ben heard a string of cuss words. Ben looked outside. Mac was wagging his finger at a young river pig who had sat on a log to pour water out of his boots.

After his swearing fit, Mac said, "You're fired," and he stomped off.

Ben asked, "What did he do wrong?"

"He sat down," Nevers said.

"He didn't talk back or nothing?"

"Nope. He just dumped the icy water out of his boots."

"No wonder Mac has a reputation for moving logs."

Once the last of the logs were in the river, Dynamite Dick loaded his jam crew in the bateau. "You got our nose bags ready?" he asked, setting a sack of dynamite in the boat.

The boys brought the lunch sacks out, and Dick passed one to each fella. "See you tonight," Dick said, pulling on his oars.

"Where they going?" Nevers asked Ben.

"The jam crew works out front. The drive crew stays with the main body of logs, and the sacking crew hangs back to take care of any logs that get stuck."

Before Dick's crew was out of sight, Slim's men picked up their nose bags and headed downstream. Most of the men walked along the bank, but gray-haired Jimmy hopped onto a log.

"Take a gander at Jimmy," Nevers pointed.

Grinning, Jimmy was riding down the river with his boots on two different logs at the same time. His knees were flexed like he was skiing, and his hair blew back under the brim of his hat.

"We gotta practice so we can do that!" Ben said.

"Let's hope we do better than him." Nevers pointed toward Klondike, who wobbled as he stepped from a log to the riverbank.

"After all his bragging, he should be dancing a jig on those logs."

Ben was amazed at how fast the fellas moved. Whether they were hopping onto a log, trotting along the shore, or steering a log with their pike poles, they stayed in constant motion.

Mike and his sacking crew started working just below the wanigan, where the last rollway had broken loose. A few logs were caught on a mud bank. A man in Mike's crew tried to turn one of the biggest logs with a cant hook, a wooden-handled tool with a hinged, metal hook, but he couldn't budge it.

"We gotta get this cork pine moving," Mike said, stepping up to his thighs in the river. Ben shivered as he looked at the freezing water. But without another word, Mike grabbed one end of the log and heaved it into the river. The splash drenched the man with the cant hook, who stared at Mike in awe.

"Let's get the rest of these stragglers into the drink," Mike said, kicking a second log in with his boot. "It don't matter how we coax 'em in. Why I remember a time when we had such a tangle of timber here that Mac was ready to call out the militia . . ."

Mike kept talking the whole time he led his crew downstream. Even after Mike's voice faded, Ben watched his hands waving like he was directing a ten-piece band.

"I've never heard a fella talk so much," Nevers said.

"It's like he's got a potful of words stoked up inside, and they keep bubbling out," Ben agreed.

"But now I see how Mike can eat ten doughnuts and ask for more," Nevers said. "He's a working fool."

Ben nodded. "And he's got the strength of four fellas."

8

Mischbrot

BEN STOOD ON THE FRONT DECK of the wanigan, watching as the last of the logs picked up speed. "You hear that?" he asked.

Nevers cocked his head. "It's rumbling like a thunderstorm."

"That's the sound of the logs bumping and scraping against each other. We'll hear that all the way to Canada."

Just then an explosion rocked the air. "Look!" Ben pointed downstream, as a spout of water shot high into the air, followed by a cloud of gray smoke that drifted over the treetops.

"Did Dynamite Dick blow himself up?" Nevers asked.

"He just blasted a splash dam that was holding back our head of water. There'll be lots more dams along the way."

"Are you two girls gonna spend your whole day holding up that railing, or you gonna work?" a voice growled from inside.

Ben turned. Sard wiped his hands on his dirty apron and squinted at them with his good eye. "I need you to fetch some flour."

"We got two barrels of Gold Medal," Ben pointed.

"That ain't real flour. I want a sack of rye."

"The men like white bread," Nevers said.

"Well that's too bad, Snicklefritz. They're getting Sard's *mischbrot* whether they like it or not."

"What's mashbrod?" Ben asked, trying to repeat the odd-sounding word.

"*Mischbrot* means mixed bread. It's my specialty. Hustle and get that flour, or you'll be swimming to catch up with us."

Once Ben and Nevers got up the bank, Nevers said, "I changed my mind about Sard. He's not a pirate, he's a mean, ugly troll."

"We should give him a chance. You're just mad 'cause he calls you Snicklefritz."

"Stop saying that stupid name, weak chin!" Nevers tightened his lips and stayed two steps ahead.

When the boys got to the store, they found that rye flour came in hundred-pound sacks. They balanced the sack on their shoulders and tried not to slip in the mud.

Ben and Nevers were halfway down the hill and panting hard, when they heard a high-pitched shriek of "*Teufel Maus!*"

"Sounds like a woman," Nevers said, hurrying across the gangplank.

"Is somebody hurt?" Ben asked.

Sard whirled around. "Don't be sneaking up on me, dummkopfs!" Then he grabbed the sack off their shoulders and carried it to the corner all by himself.

Surprised at Sard's strength, Ben couldn't help staring.

"Vat you gaping at?" Sard said.

"Nothing," Ben said.

"Shut your yap then. A closed mouth don't catch flies."

Ben saw a broken broom handle on the floor. "What happened?"

"A *Teufel Maus.*"

"A what?" Nevers asked.

"Devil mouse. He came creeping out from under the stove. I took a swing and missed."

"Why'd you call him that?" Ben asked.

"Mice are the Devil's spawn. I need another sack of flour. And get me a new broom when you're up at the store."

"Those sacks weigh a hundred pounds!" Nevers said.

"Maybe if you used your muscles more and your mouth less, you'd top a hundred pounds yourself, Snicklefritz."

When Ben started laughing, Nevers said, "Didn't Mr. Sardman tell you to keep your mouth shut?"

"Mr. Sardman!" Sard laughed. "Snicklefritz is a feisty fella. You'd better do as he says, Little Ben."

Nevers was so steamed that he didn't speak. When they got to Main Street, Ben stopped. "It's gonna be hard enough working with Sard, but if we don't stick together, it'll be twice as tough." He held out his hand. "Friends again?"

Nevers hesitated, and then he shook Ben's hand. "Maybe we should start by dunking Sard in the river."

"At least his apron would get a washing," Ben laughed.

When the boys got back with the second sack of flour and the broom, Sard was measuring sugar into a tin bowl. Ben cleared his throat so they wouldn't startle him again. Without turning, Sard said, "Put the flour in the corner."

Next Sard stirred some hot water into the bowl.

"You like your coffee that sweet?" Nevers asked.

"Vat fool would drink coffee out of a bowl?" Sard asked.

"So what are you mixing?" Ben asked.

"Watch and learn," Sard said.

After Sard mixed the sugar water, he pulled a red handkerchief out of his pocket and tore off a strip.

"Why would you rip up a good handkerchief?" Nevers asked.

Ignoring the question, Sard carried the bowl of sugar water outside and set it on the back deck railing. Then he got a hammer and three nails.

"Any idea what he's doing?" Nevers asked.

Ben shrugged as he watched Sard tack one end of the red cloth to the railing. Then Sard drove two more nails at an angle that caught the rim of the bowl and held it fast.

"There," he stepped back and admired his work.

"There what?" Nevers asked.

"You'll see," Sard said. "Now bring me that rye, and we'll get our *mischbrot* started."

Without washing his hands or measuring, Sard tossed a dozen handfuls of rye into a big mixing bowl, along with a few pinches of salt and some little seeds.

"What are those?" Ben asked.

"Caraway."

Then Sard added water, molasses, and sourdough starter to the mixing bowl. He stirred it all together and threw a towel over the top. "By morning we'll be set to bake real bread."

Ben wrinkled his nose at the bitter yeasty smell. Pa baked light, crusty bread, but Sard's dough looked dark and heavy.

When Sard was done, he wiped his hands on his filthy apron.

Ben was just thinking how upset Pa would be about Sard not washing up, when Mike stuck his head in the door and said, "It's moving time." He waved Ben and Nevers outside. "You boys better learn the routine 'cause we'll be doing this three times a day." He led them up the bank and showed them how to untie the bow and stern ropes and coil them on the decks.

"Then we pull in the gangplanks." Mike dragged the front plank onto the deck and dropped it with a crash.

"You two can take care of the rear."

Mike grinned as they struggled with the heavy plank. "Good work. Now let's get this cookshack moving!"

The wanigan drifted out from the bank with the firewood raft trailing from one side and the canoe tied to the other. Mike pointed to the rope near the back door. "We've got to keep that coil neat, 'cause we'll need it to put on the brakes later."

"Brakes?" Ben asked.

"You'll see," Mike grinned.

"Are we clear?" Sard asked.

Mike nodded at Sard. "I'll take the stern sweep if you'll handle the bow." Mike wrapped his huge hands around the twenty-foot-long oar that stuck off the back deck and pulled hard. Sard went forward to work the bow.

As the wanigan moved out into the current and picked up speed, Mike waved to two of his sacking crew and hollered, "Look out, Canada, here we come!"

Ben felt relieved to be on his way, but at the same time, he was uneasy. He looked down at the dark water rushing past the hull. Though he was finally free from his pa, with a hundred miles of wilderness between Blackwater and the border—and a strange cook as his boss—he was headed into unknown territory.

9

Under an Open Sky

THE UPPER BLACKWATER ran through a logged-over area and past a handful of homestead cabins. With the open sky above them and the river pushing them steadily north, Ben and Nevers stood on the back deck and visited with Mike.

As Mike steered, he kept up a running commentary, mixing observations of the river with random thoughts. In no particular order, he shared stories about a three-toed cat he'd owned as a boy, a haunted house, and an uncle who'd sailed on a four-masted schooner. And he recited a dozen facts about his hometown of Seney, Michigan, which sounded just as tough as Blackwater.

As Ben listened to Mike, he craned his neck to see what was coming around each bend. Standing beside Nevers reminded Ben that leaving Pa and going out on his own wasn't half as scary as what his friend faced every day. Ben looked forward to seeing Pa and Evy when his trip was done, but for Nevers, whose whole family was gone, there was no going home—not ever.

"Is that the sound of the logs again?" Nevers asked.

"That grinding and churning will be with us all the way," Mike said.

To Ben, the rumble sounded like the breathing of a giant beast waking from slumber.

When the wanigan floated through a sweeping curve, Mike waved to two more of his sacking crew that were up to their waists in the icy water. "Rassle 'em back in," he called.

Mike pointed. "There's a tricky eddy by the bank that always catches logs."

"What's an eddy?" Nevers asked.

"If there's a sharp bend or a boulder or stump sticking out, the water swirls around and moves everything back upstream."

"This is one crazy river," Nevers said. "To start off, downstream is north, which don't make no sense. Then once we get going, the current sends everything back where it came from."

"Since you're gonna be on this crazy river for the better part of two months, you'd better get used to it," Mike grinned.

"At least we finally got going," Nevers said. "I was afraid if we'd waited any longer, we'd be cooking a second breakfast."

Mike laughed. "Ain't no such thing as a second breakfast. There's first lunch and second lunch. But with our late start today, we'll have time for only one lunch. Speaking of lunches, I see you got a few of them oatmeal cookies left."

"Do you want me to get you one?" Nevers asked.

"How about if you make it a half dozen?"

Mike was chewing on his last cookie, when they passed a doe and a spotted fawn drinking at the water's edge. The doe's coat was dull and mottled from winter, and she blinked slowly as the boat drifted by. A tall spruce cast saw-toothed shadows on the bank, and the air was heavy with the scent of pine needles and thawing earth.

Farther on they passed a blue heron standing stilt-legged in the shallows. The bird's head flashed down, and he speared a fish with his bill. Tossing it into the air, he caught it in his mouth and tilted back his head to jiggle it down.

Nevers said, "I wouldn't want to get stabbed by him."

A short while later they approached a gradual bend, and Mike called out, "Ready, Sard?"

"I got her," Sard hollered back.

As the current sped up, Mike had to work the heavy oar to keep the wanigan from running into the bank. Watching the muscles stand out under Mike's wool shirt, Ben understood why it took a strong fella to handle the stern.

"We're really moving now," Ben said.

"Wait 'til we hit our first rapids," Mike said.

Just then a pair of chickadees landed on the roof of the wanigan. Ben was listening to their pure, two-note whistles, when a horrible noise came from the front deck.

"Sounds like a dying cat," Nevers said, as the startled chickadees flew off.

Mike laughed. "I see you boys don't appreciate singing."

"That's no song I ever heard," Ben said.

"It's German," Mike laughed, "I've heard Sard before. He favors old folk songs. He's never in tune, but he's got good volume."

Ben and Nevers frowned as the strange words echoed across the water: *"Ich weiß nicht, was soll es bedeuten."*

"Sounds more like throat clearing," Nevers said.

"So much for the peace and quiet of the woods," Ben said.

The river flowed through a long stretch of flat, swampy land with stunted tamarack trees on both sides. The logs ran smoothly, and the scent of pine bark lingered in the air. When the boys got bored with the scenery, they marched across the deck, testing their new calk boots.

For a short time the wanigan caught up with Jimmy and Slim. Jimmy was whistling to himself and dancing from one log to another, while Slim, with his pipe relaxed in his mouth, worked from the bank and steered a log with his pike pole.

When Sard took a break from his singing, Ben asked him the reason for the sugar bowl. But he only said, "Look and learn."

Later, while Sard was steering through a tight bend, Ben pushed a crust of bread under the stove for the meadow mouse.

"We gonna see any white water today?" Ben asked Mike. "I wish we could have a little excitement."

"Be careful with that wishing," Nevers said. "Look what you got us so far." He nodded toward the front where Sard was croaking out another German song.

"What's that supposed to mean?" Mike asked.

"Nothing," Ben said. He didn't have the heart to tell Mike that he'd wished Pa and his good cooking away.

"If you want excitement, Arrowhead Rapids is just ahead. She's pretty tame, but we'll hit a jaw-dropper farther on."

"Dead Man's Rapids?" Nevers asked.

"So even our Carolina boy has heard of Dead Man's, eh? But for now listen up."

"All I hear is Sard's sorry excuse for singing," Nevers said.

"Listen harder." Mike held his oar still.

Ben finally said, "I hear a little trickle."

Nevers nodded, "Me too." By then the sound was louder.

As the current sped up, Ben pointed to the firewood raft trailing behind them. "Will the raft be okay?"

"It's got no choice but to follow. You two should step up front and get a better view."

When Nevers hesitated, Mike grinned. "Sard won't have time to sing once we hit the white water."

As the boys walked forward, Nevers said, "Make some noise so Sard don't think we're sneaking up on him."

"Good idea." Ben coughed loudly.

When they got up front, Sard squinted at Ben with his one eye. "Why you coughing? I don't like being around germy kids."

"I'm not sick," Ben said.

Sard frowned. "Sick or not, you'd better grab something that won't rip loose. This boat will be rocking shortly."

The sound of rushing water was clear now.

"Make sure you hug the east bank," Mike called.

"We're tracking fine," Sard said.

When the head of the rapids came into view, Ben was surprised to see three-foot-high waves rolling over boulders on the right. To the left was a scary, undercut root bank that looked like it could suck a man in.

"I thought Mike said this was an easy rapids?" Ben asked.

Nevers's eyes were wide. "You wished for excitement."

"Hang on, girls!" Sard yelled, over the building roar.

The bow of the wanigan bounced up when it hit the first waves, nearly buckling Ben's knees. Then just as quickly it dipped again, as they shot down a white-water chute. Water splashed in Ben's and Nevers's faces, and they both yelled and clutched at the door frame to keep from falling over.

Sard laughed as the bow bucked up, and he steered the wanigan past a lichen-crusted boulder. When they took two more quick drops, Ben fought to keep his balance, and the water sprayed even higher.

"It's like we're riding on busted wagon springs!" Nevers shouted.

The rapids ended as quickly as they had begun. Sard was still chuckling when the wanigan drifted into a quiet pool. "You and Snicklefritz are looking pale, Little Ben."

Ben glared at Mike, who was grinning through the back door. "You said this was a tame rapids."

Before Mike could answer, a voice said, "Looks like you made her in one piece." It was Mac, waving them into shore.

The rumble downstream told Ben that they'd nearly caught up with the main body of logs.

Mike asked, "You boys want to see how we put on the brakes?"

"Sure," Ben said.

Mike and Sard worked their oars until the wanigan was a few feet from shore.

Then Mike said, "Follow me," as he walked to the front deck and jumped onto the bank.

Mike landed cleanly, but Ben and Nevers both stumbled.

"Catch!" Sard called. He'd moved to the stern to toss the mooring line. Mike grabbed the rope, ran to a big red pine, and looped two quick turns around the trunk.

"Stand clear," Mike said.

Ben watched the rope go taut as the wanigan pulled.

"Now we slow her down." Mike leaned back as the coils tightened around the tree. The dry bark crackled, and the rope squeaked, cutting deep into the wood.

"That rope is so hot it's smoking!" Nevers said.

"We almost got her," Mike said. The rope looked ready to snap, but the wanigan gradually swung into shore and stopped.

"There we go," Mike said, wrapping another quick turn around the trunk and tying a slipknot. "You gotta take care with a big boat like this. I've seen fellas lose a few fingers." Mike plucked the rope, which made a deep bass note. "Hear that tension?"

After Mike had secured the bowline, he said, "You boys can set out the gangplanks. I'll help my sacking crew toss a few logs."

Mac, who'd been watching the whole time, asked Ben, "How was your first taste of white water?"

"Fine, sir."

"You listen to Mike. He can teach you as much about this river as any—"

Before Mac could finish, Sard hollered. "Let Mac get back to work, you dunderheads! The sacking crew will be surly if we don't serve up their slop on time."

Ben saw Mac wince at the word slop. Lumberjacks took their food seriously and spoke about a fine meal for months afterward.

Before Sard started cooking lunch, he checked the sugar bowl on the back railing and refilled what had spilled in the rapids.

"You aim to tell us what that bowl is for?" Nevers asked.

"I told you to watch and learn."

For lunch, Sard served beans and wieners along with stewed prunes and some of Pa's leftover bread. Mike's crew looked disappointed with the meal, but they ate without complaining.

Ben and Nevers were still cleaning up when Sard said, "You pups need to cut more firewood. That dead jack pine on the other bank should do."

Ben nodded. He decided he would just nod at Sard instead of trying to remember which ear was his good one.

As Ben untied the canoe, Mike called, "Don't forget that canoe is just like a baby."

"I know," Ben groaned.

Nevers grabbed an axe, and Ben, a bow saw. But when they were about to climb into the canoe, Sard said, "You chuckleheads are forgetting something."

"We got the tools," Nevers said.

"But you got something else that's a problem," Sard said.

Ben and Nevers both frowned.

"Do you want that birch-bark canoe to float or not?"

Ben finally looked down at his spiked boots. "Our calks. We need our other boots so we don't punch holes in the canoe."

"I'm working with two boy geniuses," Sard shook his head.

By the time Ben and Nevers had finished splitting and stacking the firewood on the raft, Mike was back.

"Time to move on and set up camp for the night," he said.

"Seems like we just got here," Ben said.

"When we switch to a regular schedule tomorrow, we'll move the wanigan three times and you'll be cooking two lunches."

"I can hardly wait," Nevers groaned.

10

Finger Stew

LATER THAT AFTERNOON when it was time to tie up the wanigan for the evening, Mike surprised Ben by asking, "You want to take a turn at putting on the brakes?"

"I suppose." Ben tried to not sound nervous.

"You won't go and cut off your fingers, will you?"

Ben shook his head, trying not to imagine how it would feel to have his fingers crushed under that thick rope.

"I can always use a finger to flavor my stew," Sard smiled.

As soon as the hull was close enough to shore, Mike picked up the stern rope. "You set?"

Ben nodded, feeling anything but ready.

When Mike yelled, "Go!" Ben jumped to shore, caught the rope, and ran up the bank like he'd seen Mike do. Ben wanted to get to a big pine, but a balsam blocked his path. So he veered toward a sturdy-looking ash tree.

Ben wrapped the rope around the trunk. But as the slack went out of the line, he saw that he'd cinched the rope too tight. He reached out to loosen it, but Mike shouted, "Stand back!"

When the rope snapped taut, the ash bent over. Ben flinched as the rope bit into the bark, and the tree bowed even more. The rope stretched, looking ready to break.

Suddenly the ash tree's roots ripped out of the ground.

"Stay clear!" Mike yelled.

Ben stared openmouthed as the ash tree jerked forward, tearing out a small pine and a clump of alder. Then the top slid into a clump of birch. Branches snapped off the ash as it wedged between two birch trunks and flexed like a bow at full draw.

"Careful!" Mike hollered, jumping ashore. But before he reached Ben, the wanigan had stopped.

Ben stared at the big root ball of the ash. As a few loose stones clattered to the ground, he tried to hide the trembling in his voice. "I thought ash trees were strong."

Mike grinned. "It mighta held if you'd let the rope slip a little more. But ash roots run shallow."

"I messed that up something awful," Ben said.

"We're just lucky nobody got hurt," Mike said. "Besides, I'm impressed by what you just invented."

"Invented?"

"You've come up with a whole new way of logging. No saws. No axes. Just lasso a tree and let the boat do the rest."

Nevers couldn't help laughing.

Just then Mac stepped into the clearing and saw the tangle of roots and branches. "Now what's gone wrong? Did a tornado blow through here?"

This time Mike joined Nevers in laughing.

"Suppose you fools can stop cackling long enough to peel some spuds?" Sard asked.

True to his "One Pot" nickname, Sard made stew for supper. Once the spuds were in the kettle, Sard said, "Now you can pitch the tents." He waved at two tents rolled up in the corner.

"Where were you fixin' to put 'em?" Nevers asked.

"On the ground," Sard said.

"Are there any directions?" Ben asked.

"Figure it out. I'm a hash slinger, not a hotel keeper."

The boys lugged the canvas up the bank and unrolled the tents. It was tricky fitting the ridgepole to the crosspieces, but once they got the first tent up, the second one went faster.

As they walked down to the wanigan, Ben asked Nevers, "You think the fellas are gonna tease me when they see that tree ripped out of the ground?"

"You ain't never gonna hear the end of it."

"I was afraid of that."

Sard interrupted, saying, "You blockheads ain't done yet."

"We got the tents up," Nevers said.

"Even a fella with one eye can see that! The river pigs like a few balsam boughs inside to pad the ground."

Ben and Nevers walked to the edge of the woods and chopped off enough branches to line both tents. By the time they were done, Ben's nose burned from the pitch smell, and his hands were so full of sap that they stuck to everything.

The boys started to wash their hands, but Sard said, "No sense cleaning up before you build the fire."

"The stove's already going," Nevers said.

"I don't mean a stove fire, Snicklefritz. I mean a bonfire. That's how we signal the men it's time to come back for dinner."

"Can't we blow Gabriel's horn and call 'em like we did last winter?" Nevers asked.

"You're chock-full of grand ideas, ain't you?" Sard rubbed his eye patch and glared at Nevers. "The river pigs have been slogging in freezing water all day, and they need to dry out their clothes. You think they'd rather warm themselves by a fire, or have some fool blow a horn in their faces?"

The sun was low in the sky, and the horizon streaked with pink by the time Ben and Nevers had started a fire and strung up lines for the men to dry their clothes.

The river pigs straggled back to camp, wet and muddy, but

in good spirits. Everyone except Slim and Jimmy were soaked to their waists. Mike's sacking crew looked the roughest. The whole bunch had muck up to their eyeballs, and they smelled like a swamp.

Ben braced himself for teasing, but the men walked past the torn-up ash tree like it wasn't anything unusual.

"Why isn't anybody ribbing me?" Ben whispered, but Nevers could only shrug.

"Soup's on!" Sard yelled.

"You don't have to call me twice," Mike smiled.

"It better be more than soup," Klondike grumped. He looked like he'd spent most of his day in the river.

"Ain't nothing wrong with a little soup, as long as I get my beans with it," Jimmy smiled. He looked at Nevers. "When I was your age, I worked in a state of Maine camp. Every day our hash slinger cooked a big pot of beans in the bean hole. That was all we ate. Unless an ox died, then we might get a taste of oxtail soup."

"All Jimmy ever talks about is his back-East beans," Dick said. "Let's get this dishing-up line moving."

"What's a bean hole?" Nevers asked.

"A pit in the ground. The cook shoveled coals over the top of the kettle and piled dirt on it," Jimmy said.

"They cooked in the dirt?" Ben asked.

"Your pa woulda had us scrub that pot a week!" Nevers said.

"Our cook didn't clean the pot 'til spring," Jimmy said. "The seasoned iron gave those beans a wicked good flavor."

"You're lucky they didn't poison you," Mike said.

Dick looked up in surprise when a hanging sausage bumped his head. "What's this? A German meat market?"

Jimmy grinned at Sard. "You gonna decorate the walls with sauerkraut next?"

"Load your plates and move along," Sard said.

Ben could tell that the men were disappointed at the meager selection of food. Along with the stew there was only Pa's left-over bread, beans, and prunes. And for dessert, instead of making a cake or pies like the fellas were used to, Sard had baked a batch of dry molasses cookies. He tapped one on a tin plate and bragged, "They keep for a month in dry weather."

Hungry Mike stared at the table as if he were looking for something more, but Sard said, "Dish up. Food is for filling the gut. It's a waste of time to fancy it up."

Only Jimmy, who thought the beans looked exceptional, patted Ben's shoulder and said, "That's fine kitchen work, son."

Ben had decided he'd hit a patch of good luck, and that no one was going to tease him about his tree-tying accident, when Dick asked, "Suppose you could put on a demonstration for us?" Dick's slow way of talking made "demonstration" sound like it had six or seven syllables.

"A cooking demonstration?" Ben asked.

Dick winked at Mike. "No, I mean a wanigan tying-up demonstration. I hear you got a special technique." The fellas in line laughed so hard that their spoons rattled on their plates.

And the fellas were still chuckling as they took seats on logs and rocks around the fire. Mike was in such a hurry to eat that he plunked himself down on the wet moss. When Jimmy stepped in front of the fire, Mike said, "Look at that. You're so skinny your shadow ain't no thicker than a candlestick."

"At least I don't need to turn sideways to get through a barn door," Jimmy shot back.

When Klondike said, "This little spit of a river makes me lonesome for the Yukon. The first time I hiked up the Chilkoot—"

Mac cut him off, saying, "If Alaska's so great, why didn't you bring us all a bag of gold?"

Only half of the fellas lined up for seconds, which Ben took for a bad sign. Last winter at the logging camp, Pa's cooking had been so good that the men often debated how high Pa's meals ranked on their all-time list of favorites.

Ben carried the coffeepot up and refilled the tin cups, while Nevers tended to the handful of tea drinkers.

Slim, who'd been quiet, smiled at Mike and said, "I hear young Ben is working on a newfangled way of logging."

"Yep. Give this boy a wanigan and a coil of rope, and he'll harvest any sapling along this river."

As the fellas laughed again, Ben realized that the ribbing would go on for a long time. But at least he hadn't lost any fingers.

It was dark by the time the fellas finished their coffee. But getting ready for bed took only seconds. They slipped off their pants, hung them on the line, and crawled into the tents.

Standing in his soggy woolen underwear and holding his gigantic pants in both hands, Mike frowned.

"What's wrong?" Ben asked.

"I'd better not strain your rope," he said, as he walked over and hung his pants over a cedar branch.

As Jimmy crouched down to crawl into the second tent, Dick asked, "What time do you want me to wake you up tomorrow?"

Jimmy hollered, "You leave the waking to the cooks."

When Jimmy saw that Ben looked confused, he explained, "Dick has a rude habit of waking people up with dynamite."

"I never use more than a quarter stick for an alarm clock."

"What about that morning you blew the corner off the bunkhouse and spilled me onto the floor?"

"I mighta overdid it that one time," Dick grinned, showing his missing tooth. "But I didn't want you to waste your whole Sunday in bed. Sweet dreams," he said, sticking a fresh chaw of tobacco into his mouth and crawling into the tent.

Nevers made a face and said, "Ugh!"

Ben blew into the air and watched his breath turn to steam. "It's gonna be frosty tonight."

"At least we got bunks. Imagine sleeping on the cold ground in wet underwear with your face stuffed full of tobacco."

"But we also got an hour of dish washing ahead."

Nevers lowered his voice, "And we gotta sleep in the same room as that crazy German."

"Vat kind of talk is zat?" Ben said, and he and Nevers both giggled.

11

The Long Knife

"WHY YOU FUSSING over those so long?" Sard asked. "It's time to hit the hay." Though it was dark outside, Ben and Nevers were still washing the dishes.

Before Ben could answer, Sard walked to his bunk, kicked off his boots, and without bothering to undress, was soon snoring.

Ben and Nevers stared at each other. "I can't believe he went to sleep in that filthy apron," Nevers said.

"And he never even washed his face."

"Should we turn off the lantern?"

"I'm washing up first," Ben said.

"And after seeing how filthy Sard is I'm using extra soap."

Once the boys were ready for bed, Ben fed the mouse a crust of bread. Then he turned off the lantern and climbed into his bunk. Moonlight streamed through the partly opened back door and shone off the tin dishes stacked on the center table.

Sard's snoring echoed from the corner.

"That sausage smell could gag a maggot," Nevers said.

"It's lots worse up here."

"I thought your pa was a big snorer, but Sard chugs like a steam locomotive."

"He's liable to blow the tar paper off the roof. I wish—"

"Ain't you done enough damage with your wishing?"

Just then Sard sucked in a ragged breath and held it.

"Sard?" Ben whispered.

But Sard's bunk was quiet.

"Sard?" Ben asked louder.

Ben was about to get up and check, when Sard let out a big, wheezing breath.

"That was scary," Nevers said.

Sard went back to his ragged snoring. And Ben was almost asleep, when Sard drew in a breath and hung on even longer.

"There he goes again," Nevers said.

"Sard?" Ben asked. "You okay?"

Both boys climbed out of their bunks, and Ben kept saying, "Sard?" as they tiptoed over the moonlit floor.

When they reached Sard's bunk, the blankets over his chest were perfectly still. "Sard?" Ben nearly shouted.

Nevers said, "My Lord! He's gone and died!"

At that same moment Sard let out a huge whoosh that made both boys jump backwards. Ben knocked the pile of tin plates off the dishing-up table, and Nevers smacked his head against the ceiling lantern. As the plates clattered to the floor, Sard yelled in German and reached under his bunk, pulling out a big knife.

"No, Sard!" Ben yelled, as the two-foot-long blade flashed in the moonlight. "No! It's us!"

Sard stopped and lowered his knife. "Vat are you dunces doing stumbling around in the dark? I coulda run you through."

"You stopped breathing," Nevers said.

"Ain't you never heard a man snore?" Sard tossed the knife under his bunk and went right back to sleep.

Ben's heart kept pounding long after he'd lain back down.

"We'd better be careful around here," Nevers whispered from below. "We got us a crazy cook and a kitchen chock-full of knives."

"I still think we should give him a chance."

"A chance to do what! Spear us? Why can't you admit you made a mistake in wishing your pa away?"

Ben lay awake for a long time, trying to imagine why a cook would be carrying such a deadly weapon. As Ben tried to quiet his mind, Sard went back to his odd snoring. Each time Sard drew in a hoarse breath, Ben couldn't help holding his own breath, as he waited for Sard to exhale. And what made it even harder for Ben to get to sleep were the sausages that hung only inches from his face and smelled like garlic and ashes.

12

A Dose of This and a Dose of That

BEN WOKE to a harsh glare of light. His head ached, and the sausage stink was worse than ever. He felt like he'd just fallen asleep, but someone had lit the lantern, and a fire was crackling in the cookstove.

Then Ben heard water splashing outside and a coarse voice singing. He lifted his head and looked out the partly open door. The sky was dark, and a cold breeze blew in. Thick frost coated the deck, but Sard had taken off his shirt, and he was kneeling over a washbasin and soaping up his bald head, arms, and chest. Ben thought he heard one of the fellas groan up in the tents, but Sard was so loud that it was hard to tell.

Since Sard had gone to bed dirty last night, Ben was shocked to see him washing now. Ben had figured Sard for the sort of lumberjack who went months without bathing.

Still singing, Sard rinsed himself off and stood up. Then he sniffed his armpits, gave a satisfied nod, and turned toward the door. That's when Ben got a second, bigger shock. Sard's eye patch was off. And before he slid it back into place, the lamplight shined directly into Sard's injured eye. Twisted folds of skin covered the sunken place where an eye should have been.

And the skin around the eye socket looked burnt and blue-green in color.

Sard stepped inside, still drying his hairy chest with a dish towel, and shouted, "*Aufwachen* you dunderheads! Wake up!"

Talking as loud as he'd been singing, Sard asked, "Vat good are cookees that can't even stoke up a fire in the morning?" He lifted a stove lid and chunked in two pieces of wood. Then he dropped it with a loud clank.

Though Sard's eye patch was back in place, Ben couldn't forget what he'd just seen.

"Is it still night?" Nevers groaned below.

Sard walked to his bunk and pulled back his blanket. "I felt something crawling on me last night. You don't have bedbugs in this wanigan, do you?" He bent down and put his face close to the straw tick mattress.

"Pa had us clean up real good," Ben said.

At that same moment the meadow mouse stuck his nose out from under the cookstove. While Sard was still inspecting his bed, Ben got up and pushed a piece of bread under the stove.

"I hope you scrubbed everything." Sard stood. "I don't like sharing my bed with vermin." He put on his dirty shirt and apron. Then he reached under his bunk. Ben saw Nevers's eyes widen. Was Sard going for that big knife again?

Instead of a blade, Sard pulled out a small wooden box and carried it to the dishing-up table. He slid the lid back and said, "My daily dosing." He held up a bottle of Ayers Pills. "These clean my liver. And this," he touched a Syrup of Figs bottle, "keeps me from getting a cold, headache, or fever. But Cascarets are my favorite." He rattled a small tin. "They cure constipation, lazy liver, worms, and bad blood."

"What about that one?" Nevers pointed at a bottle of Hinkley's Bone Liniment.

"The slogan says it all," Sard said.

"Good for man or beast," Ben read.

"I figure I'm covered either way," Sard laughed.

Ben kept staring at Sard's eye patch. He wanted to ask how he got injured, but he knew it wasn't polite.

Sard tossed the pills into his mouth and chased them down with a teaspoon of Syrup of Figs. Then he burped and said, "Are you boneheads ready to boil up breakfast?"

Without waiting for an answer, he said, "First off we'll get my *mischbrot* baking. The river pigs will need something to fill their nose bags for lunch. Get that bowl, Snicklefritz. I'll show you girls how to make real bread."

"We'd better wash up first," Ben said.

Nevers grabbed a towel and a bar of soap while Ben refilled the washbasin and carried it outside. The boys knelt and washed their hands and faces, but no matter how hard they scrubbed, yesterday's balsam sap wouldn't come off.

"Brrr . . . it's freezing," Nevers's teeth chattered as he rubbed his sticky palms together.

"I saw Sard's eye," Ben whispered.

"No fooling? Is it all bloody?"

"The skin's scarred and wrinkled. And the bone looks smashed. It's an awful mess."

"I hope I never have to see it," Nevers said.

"No wonder we're cold," Ben said, pointing at the skim of ice along the shore. He imagined how warm it would be back at Evy's house this morning. He hoped Pa was doing okay. Up the bank, curls of smoke rose from the coals of last night's bonfire. And snores of various pitches issued from the tents.

Before they went back inside, Nevers whispered, "I'm hankering to ask Sard what he's doing with that big knife."

"I wouldn't want to make him mad."

"With all those pills he's taking, do you reckon he's a hypocrite?"

Ben smiled. "You mean hypochondriac—a fella who worries too much about being sick."

As soon as the boys got back inside, Sard took the towel off the bread bowl and gave the dough a poke. Then, tearing off a hunk, he folded the corners, patted it into a round loaf, and plopped it on the counter. "That's all there is to it. After the loaves rise, we'll sprinkle on some cornmeal, and bake 'em up."

Sard tossed a hunk of dough to Ben. "Give it a try, Little Ben."

"Y'all want me to get the bread pans?" Nevers asked.

"Didn't I tell you to stop that yawling and talk English? I never in my life have seen two pups with so many questions. You don't bake round loaves in pans, but we need a splash of water in one pan to make steam so the crust firms up."

When Sard said he was boiling breakfast, he was serious. He made a big pot of boiled oatmeal and heavy doughnuts, which he boiled—Sard's word for deep-frying—in lard. Plus he warmed up beans and stewed prunes, which lumberjacks expect with every meal.

When Sard stirred leftover potatoes into his doughnut batter, Nevers stared. "Sure you want taters in there? The fellas like their taters separate."

"Well, the fellas ain't cooking, are they? Putting the spuds in the doughnuts saves dirtying another pan."

The more Ben saw of Sard's cooking, the more he understood why "One Pot" was a perfect nickname.

Sard dropped his doughnut batter onto the counter and flattened it with his hands. Then he tossed the doughnut cutter to Ben. "Make yourself useful."

By four thirty the doughnuts were out of the frying pan, and the rye bread was cooling on the table. Sard turned to Ben, "Call those river pigs down for their swill." Then he pitched Nevers a bread knife, saying, "Catch, Snicklefritz."

"Yikes!" Nevers caught the wooden handle.

"Just testing your reflexes," Sard laughed. "Hack off some bread."

Grateful that Sard wasn't throwing knives at him, Ben stepped onto the deck to yell, "Come and get it." But Hungry Mike was already tromping across the gangplank with Jimmy and the rest of the crew jostling in line behind him. The fellas' pants were still wet, and everyone smelled of smoke from the bonfire. But to Ben the stink of the wet wool and wood smoke was an improvement over the sausages he had to sleep by.

Most of the men were silent and glum. But Jimmy grinned as he greeted Ben. "'Tis a fine day for running logs, Master Ward."

As cold and dark as it was, Jimmy's good humor amazed Ben.

Ben dished up the food while Nevers sliced the bread as fast as he could.

Once the fellas were seated on the riverbank, Ben carried up the coffeepot.

Mike was studying the stack of doughnuts on his plate. He picked up one. "This has got a suspicious amount of heft."

"They're good enough if you heap your beans on top," Jimmy said. His plate was already half empty.

"It's the potatoes," Ben said.

"I didn't get no spuds," Mike said, looking at the other plates to see if he'd missed something.

"There's potatoes in the doughnuts," Ben said.

"No," Mike said. "Who woulda ever thought?"

In spite of his long face, Mike managed to eat all of his doughnuts and go back for seconds.

The men polished off their breakfast in only a few minutes. Then Jimmy said, "Time to lard up."

When Ben went inside to get the lard, Sard handed him the

can he'd used for cooking. But Ben said, "I'll take the same can the fellas used yesterday. We don't want to mix up the eating lard with the feet lard."

"If you're gonna be picky, help yourself," Sard said.

Joking in the frosty air, the men stripped off their pants and long underwear, and coated their steaming legs and feet with lard. Since it was colder than yesterday, most of the fellas larded all the way up to their waists.

"It's colder than Fairbanks!" Klondike whined.

But Jimmy only grinned. "I've never been one to complain about the weather. I figure a fella can change his socks or his pants. He can even take a shot at changing his life—I've given that a go a time or two—but there ain't no way to change the weather. So you may as well take what you get."

"Amen," Dick said, spitting tobacco juice through his missing front tooth and onto the frosty ground.

Nevers grimaced and stepped sideways to avoid the spit, but Dick said, "Stop right there."

"What did I do?"

"Just set your boot next to Mike's bare foot."

Being careful to not bump the ugly scar where Mike's little toes used to be, Nevers lined up his boot with Mike's foot. "I knew it," Dick said. "Look here, fellas. Mike's foot is bigger than Nevers's boot!"

Everyone stared at Mike's enormous foot.

"Those feet are as big as snowshoes," Jimmy chuckled.

"That ain't fair," Mike said. "Dick picked the littlest fella around. Set your boot here, Ben."

Ben tried to avoid looking at Mike's toes, as he slid his boot forward, while Mike kept talking to Dick and Jimmy. "You two won't be so quick to sound off now."

But Dick punched Mike's shoulder. "Your foot's a good two inches longer than Ben's boot! Those ain't feet, they're skis!"

"If they was boats, you could float yourself all the way to Canada," Jimmy said, and the fellas all laughed.

After the men got their pants back on, Ben and Nevers passed out the nose bags, which they'd filled with bread and sausage and cookies.

The drive crew slung their bags over their shoulders and followed Slim along the bank. At the same time Dynamite Dick loaded his jam crew into the bateau and rowed out ahead of the logs. As usual, Mike's sacking crew started their day by heading back upstream to check for stranded logs.

Just beyond the wanigan, Mike saw two logs stuck against the bank. "The pike poles won't help with all this ice," Mike said, as he and another fella stepped into the river, breaking the ice with a loud crunch. Then they pitched both logs into the river.

Nevers, who was shivering beside Ben, said, "I'll take kitchen work over ice breaking any day."

"I won't argue that," Ben said.

13

Call Him Lucky

WHEN THE SACKING CREW CAME BACK for their first lunch, Ben braced himself for more teasing over his wanigan-tying accident, but no one said a thing. And after Mike helped them move the wanigan, he pointed to the stern rope and asked, "You ready?"

"For what?" Ben expected a smart remark.

"You know the routine. Pick a tree, and give it another go."

Ben waited for the punch line, but nothing else came. "Get up front, and we'll swing her in," Mike said.

This time Ben chose a solid pine tree in clear view, and he tied off the wanigan just like he'd seen Mike do.

"Got all your fingers?" Mike called.

Ben grinned and held up both his hands.

"Good job. We'll let Nevers try next time."

Along with practicing their raisin spitting, Ben and Nevers tested their calk boots every chance they got. When they were on the deck, they clumped across the planks, imagining they were full-fledged log drivers. And when they were on the riverbank, they picked out a log and walked the length of it, pretending they were shooting a mean stretch of rapids.

Late that afternoon Ben and Nevers were on the bank,

splitting kindling for starting fires, when Nevers hopped onto a moss-covered log to test his balance.

Sard growled, "This ain't playtime, Snicklefritz."

"Looks like we got two gents who are ready for log riding," someone called.

Ben and Nevers turned. Mike and his crew were back.

Nevers pointed at his spikes. "These'll stick to anything."

Mike smiled. "If you boys want to test those calks, there's a log around the corner you can try."

"Aren't you gonna have lunch first?" Ben asked.

"This won't take but a minute." Mike showed them a big log with one end stuck on the bank. "The wide ones are real stable."

"I'll try her," Ben said.

With Mike's crew watching, Ben stepped off the bank. When the log didn't budge, he took another step.

"Hurry up so I can have a turn," Nevers said.

Ben walked to the far end, grinning. "Nothing to it," he said. But as he turned to start back, the log lifted off the bank.

Mike grinned, as Ben took a step toward shore, and the log started spinning. "Wooooo!" Ben yelled. The log spun faster, and his left boot caught, pitching him face first into the water. The shock took his breath away, and his skin burned from the cold.

The fellas all roared.

Ben waded to the bank, shivering. Mike extended a hand and helped him up. "You ready to join Slim's crew?"

"Nnnnot yyyyet," Ben's teeth chattered as the men kept laughing. Freezing water sloshed in his boots as he walked back to the wanigan.

Mike looked at Ben. "We need to fix those calks."

"What do you mean?" His numb lips made it hard to talk.

Mike turned to Sard. "You got an ice pick?"

"I know just vat you need." Sard came back with an ice pick and a hammer.

"Have a seat, and hand me those boots," Mike said.

As soon as Ben's boot was off, Mike set the point of the ice pick inside it and raised the hammer.

"You're not gonna put a hole in my new boot?"

"I am," Mike said.

A half-dozen holes later, Mike held up the boot, and water trickled out. "Now it'll drain like it should."

Mike finished Ben's boots and held out his hand for Nevers's.

"But they're brand new," Nevers pleaded.

"A river man's gotta have proper foot gear."

After Mike left, Ben spoke to Nevers. "I knew river pigs were tough, but after being in that freezing water, I can't believe they wade all day long."

"Plus they're sleeping in wet underwear," Nevers said.

Despite Ben's spill, the boys kept practicing on logs that were wedged against the shore.

Every time they tried a log, Sard said, "You clowns are gonna take another bath." But after a short while, both Ben and Nevers could balance on a free-floating log.

"Pretty soon we'll be birling like Slim," Nevers bragged.

"Let's not get ahead of ourselves," Ben said.

Ben and Nevers also improved their raisin spitting to the point where they were hitting the bucket with every third or fourth shot and feeling proud.

But when Mike got back early one afternoon and saw the raisins in the bucket, he frowned. "What you doing?"

"Getting ready for a raisin-spitting contest," Ben said.

Mike laughed. "We don't never have those with Dick around."

"How come?" Nevers asked.

"I'll show you later on."

When the crews got back that evening, Mike called to Sard, "Send your cookees out, and tell 'em to bring a few raisins."

"What's up?" Mac asked, as Jimmy and the other fellas gathered along the shore.

Mike said, "Young Ben and his partner are looking for a raisin-spitting lesson."

Ben and Nevers set their bucket on the deck, and Mike turned to Dick, "You ready?"

"I need a target," Dick drawled in his superslow way.

"We got one," Ben pointed to the bucket.

Dick shook his head. "Might as well use a washtub." Ducking inside the wanigan, Dick came out with a tin coffee cup, which he placed on the deck railing. Then he stepped back three paces.

"You're not gonna shoot at that little thing?" Nevers asked.

Dick grinned, showing his brown teeth. "You got those raisins?"

Ben opened his palm.

"One'll do," Dick said. After taking his slimy chaw of tobacco out and setting it on the railing, Dick popped a raisin into his mouth.

Ben saw that the men onshore were all smiling.

As Dick took aim, Nevers whispered to Ben, "Ain't no way he's hitting a target that small."

Before Ben could agree, Dick lifted his chin and spat.

All eyes followed the raisin as it flew across the deck in a graceful arc, spinning end over end until it hit the bottom of the cup with a loud plink.

The fellas on the bank cheered.

"I ain't never seen the likes of it!" Nevers said.

"Ole Dick don't miss," Jimmy said.

Ben stared at Dick. "How'd you learn to do that?"

Dick put his chaw back in his mouth and shrugged like he hadn't done anything special. "From the time I was a little tyke I've had a talent for spitting. Didn't matter whether I was aiming for a doodlebug or a tin can, I nailed it every time."

"I could practice a year and never make a shot like that."

Nevers looked at Ben. "So much for your bright ideas about

raisin-spitting contests," he picked up the bucket. "We won't need this no more."

That night Ben was so tired he fell asleep before Sard started snoring. The next thing he knew Nevers was poking him.

"Is it morning?" Ben asked.

"Look," Nevers whispered, pointing toward Sard's bunk.

Ben craned his neck to see into the corner. Moonlight streamed through the partly open door. He couldn't believe his eyes. The meadow mouse was sitting on Sard's chest and riding his blanket as it rose and fell. Then the mouse wiggled his tail and sniffed Sard's beard.

"He must be looking for crumbs in his whiskers," Ben said.

"That mouse is a goner if Sard wakes up."

"I was hoping we could keep him as a pet, but we gotta get him off this boat," Ben said.

"How?"

Ben tiptoed to the counter, grabbed a cookie, and handed Nevers a pot with a lid. Then the boys snuck over to Sard's bunk and crouched down. Nevers tilted the pot, while Ben dropped a trail of cookie crumbs across Sard's blanket. At first the mouse wouldn't leave Sard's beard. But he finally turned and snatched a piece of cookie.

When the mouse hopped to a second crumb, Sard coughed in his sleep. The boys ducked down, and Ben found himself staring at the hilt of Sard's big knife. He tried not to think of what Sard might do if he woke up with a mouse on his chest.

The boys waited until Sard's breathing evened out. Then they lured the mouse closer with more cookie crumbs. When Ben dropped the last of the cookie into the pot, the mouse hopped after it.

Nevers slipped on the lid and carried the pot to the door. Ben could hear the mouse nibbling inside. Sard coughed again, and they froze until he settled down.

The boys crept across the deck, carried the pot to the edge

of the woods, and tipped it on its side. The mouse hopped out, holding one last piece of cookie in his paws.

"Go find yourself a girlfriend," Ben whispered.

"But don't go crazy over a gal like some fellas do."

As the mouse hopped away, Ben said, "It's too bad we couldn't keep him."

"It was way too risky."

Ben nodded. "But after snacking off Sard's beard and surviving, I figure he's already earned himself a name."

"What might that be?"

"Lucky," Ben said, as he and Nevers smiled in the moonlight.

14

The Mystery of the Sugar Bowl

THE FARTHER NORTH the men pushed the logs, the more lonesome Ben got. One morning when Dick blew out a dam on a feeder stream, the smoke cloud reminded Ben of the day he'd said good-bye to Pa and Evy. Though Ben joined Nevers in joking about how silly Pa and Charlie had acted, Ben was more worried than he let on.

Pa had always been rock steady. If he had a fault, it was in being too predictable and boring. He was the last man in the world Ben would've picked to squabble over a woman. Ben wondered if he'd ever get his old Pa back.

After a week on the river, Ben was tuckered out from getting up at three o'clock and working past dark. When he and Nevers weren't cooking or washing the dishes, they were fetching water, and when they weren't fetching water, they were setting up camp, cutting wood, or doing the laundry, though Sard thought washing clothes was a waste of time.

One afternoon when the boys were on the deck, washing the dish towels, Sard called from inside, "Why waste the soap? They'll just get dirty again."

Nevers whispered to Ben, "We might be as busy as a pair

of stump-tailed cows in fly time, but we don't want our towels looking like his apron."

"That's for sure," Ben said, thinking fondly of how clean Pa kept his kitchen.

One job Ben enjoyed was starting the bonfire each night. And setting up the tents wasn't bad. But he hated cutting the balsam boughs, which left his hands permanently sticky with sap.

After they parked for the night, Ben challenged Nevers to a contest to see who could pitch a tent the fastest. "We'll each take one, and the loser has to line both tents with boughs."

"You're on," Nevers said.

Ben got off to a quick start, and he had his tent up before Nevers had tied off his last rope.

Ben stood with his arms folded, smiling until Nevers was done. Then Ben handed him the hatchet. "Have fun chopping."

"Not so fast."

"What do you mean?"

"Have a look."

When Ben turned, he saw that two of his stakes had pulled loose, and his tent was slowly collapsing.

"Make sure you pick out lots of nice soft boughs for the fellas," Nevers said, handing the hatchet back to Ben.

The next morning, they were almost done cooking breakfast when Ben heard a loud metal banging.

"What's that ruckus?" Nevers asked.

"Sounds like somebody's hammering on the stovepipe." But when Ben slid the back door open, the banging stopped. He stepped outside. "There's nothing out here."

"You got rocks in your head," Sard laughed.

But the "Rat, tat, tat, tat . . ." started up again. This time it was coming from the back wall.

Ben stuck his head outside. "It's a woodpecker hitting the washtub!"

Nevers joined Ben. "And he's a big one!"

After one more spurt of hammering, the woodpecker squawked and flew across the river.

Ben shook his head. "That bird must be crazy."

"No crazier than you," Sard said. "He's just drumming on the loudest thing he can find to attract a lady friend."

"You reckon he'd get a headache," Nevers said.

"They got hard heads," Sard said. "And the louder they drum, the more the lady woodpeckers love it."

"Is that why you sing all the time?" Nevers asked Sard. "Are you practicing to attract a lady friend?"

"I got no patience for women. I sing to wake myself up. Plus singing is good for the soul. A famous fella once said, 'Without music, life would be a mistake.'"

Jimmy, who had stepped onto the deck, said, "If you ask me, calling your morning croaking music is a bigger mistake."

"Well, nobody asked you," Sard said. Then turning to Nevers, he added, "Load some beans on Jimmy's plate so he stops yapping."

Later that morning when Mike came back to move the wanigan, he stopped and stared at something.

"Is that big woodpecker back?" Ben asked.

"See for yourself," Mike whispered.

Ben peeked out the door. A little bird with a ruby throat and a button-sized head was perched on the rim of Sard's tin bowl and dipping his thin beak into the sugar water.

"I'd forgotten about that sugar bowl," Ben said.

"A hummingbird," Nevers whispered, as the little bird flicked his tongue into the sugar water.

Sard joined them. "I see our neighbors are back."

The bird dipped down for a last sip and then darted off with a high-pitched chirp, its wings buzzing.

Mike looked at Sard. "I never figured you for the sort to feed hummingbirds."

"I like feeding birds 'cause I can give 'em the same recipe every day, and they don't complain."

"Well, I wouldn't last too long on sugar water."

By that afternoon a half-dozen hummingbirds were buzzing around the deck. Sard waved Nevers over. "I'll show you a trick."

"What you gonna do?"

"Just hold out your hand."

He reached out gingerly, and Sard spooned some sugar water into Nevers's palm. Then he said, "Set your hand on the railing."

Nevers put his hand next to the bowl, but a hummingbird flew off. "I scared him."

"Hold real still," Sard said.

Soon another hummingbird flew down and took a drink from the bowl. At the same time a second bird flitted back and forth over Nevers's hand. Then it dipped down for a nervous drink. When Nevers didn't move, the bird perched at the base of his thumb and drank again. "It tickles," Nevers whispered.

When Ben took a turn, a bird landed on his hand. And he marveled at the iridescent green feathers. "It's so light it feels like there's no weight at all."

Ben was about to thank Sard, but before he had a chance, Sard said, "Speaking of birds. You bird brains better stoke up our stove so we can warm some slop for the river pigs."

Ben sighed. Whenever Sard seemed ready to show a hint of kindness, he always snapped back to his old, ornery self.

15

The Sweepers

BEN WOKE to the greasy stench of garlic sausage. As the sun
gradually increased in power, the days grew longer and warmer.
The deck was free of frost in the morning, and the sacking crew
no longer had to break ice. But Sard's sausages made Ben's
bunk the smelliest place in the wanigan.

The night before, Ben had heard the men grumbling about
Sard's cooking. Dick told Mike, "I'm seeing black bread and
sausages in my sleep."

Mike nodded. "That German's showed us a mediocre exhibi-
tion of hash slinging so far."

Ben and Nevers had both hinted to Sard that the men would
appreciate more variety, but Sard only said, "This is a wanigan,
not some fancy hotel."

The food was always the same. Along with the rye bread,
beans, and stewed prunes that came with every meal, Sard
served oatmeal and doughnuts for breakfast, wieners for lunch,
and stew for supper. Dessert was always his rock-hard molasses
cookies.

Later that morning, as the river pigs were larding up, Jimmy
warned, "We'd better be on the lookout for sweepers today."

"What's a sweeper?" Nevers asked.

Mike was about to say something, when Jimmy smiled and

said, "The only sweeping you need to worry about is working your broom."

Ben and Nevers were cleaning up after the second lunch, when Mike said, "There's a couple of logs right below here if you care to practice your riding skills."

"No tricks this time?" Ben asked.

"You ready for real log riding or not?" Mike asked.

Mike showed Ben and Nevers two broad pine logs. He hooked one with his pike pole and held it steady.

Ben stepped on to test it. "It's rock solid."

"A grandma could ride that log," Mike said.

He pulled in a second log for Nevers. Then he gave both logs a nudge with his pole and eased them into the current. "We'll catch you around that bend."

"Don't we need pike poles?" Ben asked.

"We'll see you below," Mike said, leading his crew along the shore. Ben was surprised to see Sard walking with them.

"Ain't this grand?" Nevers said, as the logs picked up speed.

Ben held his arms out for balance, but the log was so stable it barely wobbled.

"Look at me," Nevers called, taking two steps forward and then edging back to the middle of his log.

The boys were moving at a good clip when they reached the bend. Mac was waiting along with Sard and the other fellas. Ben couldn't understand why everyone was watching until he saw a low birch tree hanging over the water.

"You see what a sweeper is now?" Jimmy called.

"What do we do?" Nevers shouted.

The tree loomed closer. Ben's mind raced. He wanted to jump for another log. But nothing was close.

"Look out!" Nevers shouted.

As Ben turned, the birch tree caught his shoulder and

knocked him into the river. The cold was a shock, and Ben spit out water and gasped, as everyone laughed.

"Help!" Nevers yelled.

Ben looked back. Nevers had grabbed the tree with his arms and hooked one leg over it. But when he tried to swing his other leg up, the seat of his pants had soaked up too much water.

"Help!" Nevers called again, as his pants got heavier.

The fellas laughed, as Nevers's pants dragged him lower and lower. And they all clapped when he finally fell into the river.

When Nevers came up sputtering, Sard called, "You shoulda larded up if you planned on going swimming, Snicklefritz."

At bedtime Ben's and Nevers's pants were still wet. So instead of hanging them on the end of the bunk, Ben draped both pairs over the line by the campfire.

The following morning when Ben brought the pants down to the wanigan, Nevers pointed at the legs. "Take a gander at that."

"They still wet?" Ben looked down and smiled. The legs of both pants had been shortened. "Somebody worked overtime last night."

"I wonder who done it."

"I'll bet it was Mike," Ben said.

Ben pulled on his pants and checked the length. "Whoever cut these off staged 'em just right."

Nevers slipped his on. "My ankles feel a might drafty."

The whole time Ben and Nevers dished up breakfast, they pretended that nothing had happened. The fellas gave them a few sideways glances, but no one said anything.

When larding-up time came, Mike finally said, "Looks like you boys sawed off your pants' legs."

"I knew it was you," Ben said.

"I didn't mess with them."

"Did you?" Ben turned to Jimmy.

"Warn't me neither."

Before Ben could ask anyone else, Sard started laughing.

Ben frowned. "It was you?"

"I figured if you dunces were pretending to be log drivers, you needed proper pants," Sard said.

"Staged pants or not," Jimmy said, "don't think for a minute we ain't got more dunkings planned for you."

"At least our pants will dry out faster next time," Nevers said.

16

Now You See It, Now You Don't

THE NEXT MORNING Ben lay in bed with his eyes closed and his ears covered to block out Sard's singing. But he still heard a buzzing sound. "Cut it out," he said to Nevers.

"Cut what out?"

Ben opened his eyes. A hummingbird was flying in tight circles over his head. Ben stared as the bird chirped loudly and then whizzed out the back door.

Sard stuck his head inside. "Get up, you laggards! That bird's letting you know her bowl is empty. Boil some breakfast for her." Then he went back to singing. Ben was glad that Sard had his eye patch on.

Nevers swung his feet to the floor and rubbed his eyes. "As if we don't have enough chores already, now we got to add bird feeding to our list."

"At least the birds don't call us names," Ben said.

"Name calling don't bother me," Nevers yawned. "Being called a dummkopf hurts a lot less than getting cracked with a stick of stove wood by my pa."

"Sorry you had it so rough."

"That's how I learned to move so quick," Nevers smiled. "Is it just me, or is Sard's singing getting louder?"

"He's getting louder and badder," Ben said.

"Badder ain't a real word. But it fits his singing."

Before Ben had the sugar water heated, Sard was back. "Finish up that bird food, numskulls," he yelled. "Two tentfuls of hungry river pigs will be tramping down here shortly."

For the rest of the morning, Sard had the boys jump from one job to another, never giving them a chance to catch their breath. And Sard seemed crabbier than usual. Once when he couldn't hear Ben, he hollered, "Talk to my good side, you ninny!"

Ben was ready to snap back, but Nevers whispered, "Tell him the truth. He ain't got a good side."

Despite Sard's grumping, the day went lightning fast. To Ben, it seemed like they had just started their first wanigan move when it was time to pitch the tents and set up camp.

It wasn't until after the boys had rinsed the supper dishes, and they were standing on the back deck that Ben noticed the sky.

"Look over there," Ben pointed west.

"Sure is pretty," Nevers whistled softly.

Above the treetops, the sky was streaked with pale blue and pink that darkened to a deep violet higher up. A breeze skittered across the water, and for a moment the white-hot embers of the campfire on the bank flickered red. The voices of the men had quieted inside the tents, and the world was perfectly still.

Just then Sard came out and hung a wet towel over the railing. Ben expected him to say something sarcastic, but Sard looked into the river and said, "Ain't it something how water reflects the colors of the sky? When you look down on a quiet evening like this, it almost feels like you're floating on the clouds."

Ben waited for Sard to follow up with a smart remark, but he stayed serious: "Vat I like most about rivers is their mystery.

A fella can never really see a river, you know, even when he's staring straight into it."

"That don't make sense," Nevers said. "The river's right there."

"I think Sard means the water is moving and changing so fast, that by the time you see it, it's gone."

"That's how it is," Sard nodded. "A fella named Heraclitus said it best: 'You can never step into the same river, for new waters are always flowing on to you.'"

Nevers asked, "Was this Heraclitus a logger or a river pig?"

"Neither. He was a philosopher. A real deep thinker."

"From back East like Jimmy?" Nevers asked.

Sard chuckled. "Lots further back than that, Snicklefritz. He lived in Greece two thousand years ago."

Ben shook his head as he watched the darkening sky. How could Sard act so ignorant and mean one minute, and then turn around and spout out quotes by dead folks that no one had ever heard of?

17

Better Than an Empty Pot

As SPRING DREW ON, Ben enjoyed waking to birdsong. New birds showed up nearly every day. The first songs started when the sky was still gray, and the chorus gradually built. But all too soon Sard's singing drowned out the music and signaled that it was time to get up and "boil some breakfast."

One morning when Ben carried the dishwater out, he noticed a hummingbird sitting on a steel hook under the eave. The bird had wrapped strands of spider silk and moss around the hook.

"Is that bird doing what I think she is?" Ben asked Sard.

"She's getting a nest ready for sure. I'll warn the fellas so they don't stomp too loud coming in."

All of the men agreed to be quiet except for Klondike, who said, "Wasting good sugar on birds is bad enough, but a fella shouldn't have to tiptoe his way to dinner."

But Mike said, "You look out for that bird, or I'll hang you on that hook."

Ben enjoyed watching the hummingbird build her nest. In less than a week she shaped it into a little cup about an inch and a half across and lined it with cattail fluff.

Shortly after the nest was finished, two cream-colored eggs appeared. Nevers stared at the jelly bean–sized eggs. "How can a baby bird come out of something that small?"

"She ain't hatching an ostrich, Snicklefritz," Sard said.

From then on, the men took extra care to be quiet when they lined up for meals. Ben noticed that Klondike even snuck a peek at the nest when he thought no one was looking.

One morning when they were getting ready to move the wanigan, Ben said, "We're running so low on flour that we might have to switch over to Gold Medal pretty soon."

Mike's eyes lit up at the thought of white bread.

"There's two little towns between us and the border," Sard said. "One of 'em should have real flour."

Later that afternoon Mike's hopes for an improvement in his diet rose again when they parked near a homestead. Sard said, "I'll see if I can buy us some eggs and a few chickens."

"Some fried chicken would taste mighty fine," Mike said.

Sard took out the coin purse that Mac had left with him, and he and the boys walked up to a weather-beaten log cabin. Behind the cabin a man and a woman were clearing a field for planting.

Sard introduced himself and got right down to business. "We'd like to buy a couple dozen eggs and a few chickens if you can spare 'em."

The fella quoted a price for the eggs, and Sard asked, "Do you have yourself a golden hen around here?"

"Of course not," the fella said.

"I didn't think so," Sard said. "Which means you shouldn't be pricing your eggs like they was solid gold."

The fella and Sard haggled for a while. The man said there was no road to his homestead, and he had to haul everything on his back. And Sard said, "An egg's an egg no matter how far the chicken that laid it had to be carried."

They settled on a price that included the man's wife catching four chickens and chopping off their heads. Ben appreciated getting the messiest part of the butchering out of the way.

"Mike's gonna be as happy as a pig in a peach orchard," Nevers said, as they lugged the chickens and a pail full of eggs back to the wanigan.

After the boys plucked the chickens, Sard said, "Don't bother to cut them up."

"You gonna fry 'em whole?" Ben asked.

"We're stewing these birds," Sard said.

"The fellas had a hankering for fried chicken," Nevers said.

"That'd be a waste," Sard said. "We'll get a couple of meals out of 'em if we make a pot of stew."

That evening Mike stepped onto the deck smiling. "So how's the apron crew? I was just telling the fellas there's nothing sweeter than the smell of chicken sizzling in an iron skillet."

Ben thought about warning Mike before he came inside, but Mike had already seen the pot bubbling. "What we got here?" He stepped forward and lifted the lid. Mike stared for a long time. "Chicken stew?" he finally said, looking like he could cry.

"And I made my special rye dumplings," Sard said.

"I was hoping for fresh fried chicken," Mike said, "but I guess a pot of boiled chicken is better than—"

"Better than an empty pot?" Nevers said.

"That's it," Mike nodded.

While the men were eating supper, the breeze died down, and clouds of tiny bugs swarmed over the camp. They flew up Ben's nose, landed in his ears, and bit him on the back of his neck.

"What kind of critters are these?" Nevers asked, as he brushed off his face and stepped closer to the fire so the smoke would keep the bugs away.

"Blackflies," Ben said.

Nevers smashed one on his forearm and looked closer. "We got some bugs like this back in Carolina. We call 'em buffalo gnats, but they ain't near so bloodthirsty."

"Since blackflies don't buzz like mosquitoes, they really sneak up on you." Ben slapped the back of his hand, leaving a splat of blood. "And they chew like wolves."

The next morning after breakfast the bugs were worse than ever. But Jimmy didn't seem to notice them, declaring as he always did, "'Tis a fine day for driving logs." But then he turned to Ben and added, "But I do need to borrow a hunk of bacon."

"There's already bacon in your beans," Ben said.

"I want a fresh piece," Jimmy said.

"It ain't healthy to eat raw bacon," Nevers said.

"'Tain't for eating. Just slice me a hunk."

Jimmy rubbed the bacon over his neck and behind his ears.

When Nevers stared, Jimmy said, "Bacon's the best bug dope you can find. Want to try some?"

Nevers shook his head. But half of the fellas smeared it on.

"Bacon gets ripe on a hot day," Dick said, "but it's better than letting the bugs chaw you up."

After the fellas left, Nevers said, "I ain't never seen fellas go through so much pig fat. First they smear lard on their feet. Then they rub bacon on their faces. What's next?"

"Maybe they'll be hanging sausages from their ears?"

Sard was the only one who wasn't bothered by the blackflies. When one landed on his arm, he ignored it.

"You just gonna let him bite you?" Nevers asked.

"A critter that small can't do much damage."

Later Nevers told Ben, "That fly chewed on Sard a good long time and never left a welt."

"His hide's so tough that bug probably broke its teeth."

18

Dead Man's Rapids

THE NEXT MORNING as Ben and Nevers untied the wanigan for their first move of the day, Ben paused to admire the wild flowers on the riverbank. Marsh marigolds brightened the river's edge, while wild strawberries and white trillium blossomed on the higher ground. The perfume in the air reminded Ben of Evy's garden back home. Pa always said that her yard was the "prettiest patch of color in the county."

"Moving this boat keeps us as busy as two moths in a mitten," Nevers said, coiling the bow rope.

"Even if we've got an arm-long list of chores, I look forward to seeing what's downriver every day," Ben said.

Ben felt a sense of adventure each time they started out. Every bend revealed something new: a partridge drumming on a log, a red-tailed hawk perched on a dead treetop, a dogwood blossom glistening with dew.

The moments Ben enjoyed most were the rare times when Sard wasn't singing. Ben loved listening to the sounds of the river. Along with the distant rumbling of the logs, the water had a music all its own. And the song constantly changed as it chattered over the rocks and whispered against the hull of the wanigan.

Though Mike didn't sing like Sard did, his constant chatter when he was steering made almost as much noise.

"That Mike sure is a talker," Nevers said.

Ben nodded. "Words are like fuel to him. Talking tires some folks out, but for Mike the more he talks, the harder he works."

Shortly after they got going, Mike told one of his stories.

"I owned a dog once," Mike began. "He was a real sad critter."

"What was so sad about him?" Ben asked.

"He had a bad accident when he was just a pup. He wandered onto the railroad tracks and got half his tail cut off. So I named him Wholesale."

"Whatever for?" Nevers asked.

"I called him Wholesale 'cause he needed to be re-tailed. Ha, ha, ha . . . And you thought the only joke I knew was the one about the canoe and the baby!"

After Mike caught his breath, he lowered his voice and switched over to his favorite subject, food. He asked Ben, "You know them beans you been serving?"

"What about 'em?"

"That's bacon you stir in, right?"

"And molasses."

"Is there any chance you could brown the bacon before you put it in the pot? Even good bacon turns mealy when you boil it."

"We told Sard the same thing," Ben said, "but he's partial to one-pot cooking."

"Lord save us," Mike sighed deep and sad.

For three days in a row the weather stayed warm and clear. The aspen trees began leafing out, and the new growth on the willows was a shiny green.

The river ran as calm and peaceful as the weather. But the gentle current bored Ben. Other than Dick blasting one splash dam, and the wanigan nearly going aground on a gravel shoal, there hadn't been any excitement.

"I wish we could see some more white water," Ben said.

"Be careful with your wishing," Nevers said.

"Whether he's wishing or not," Mike said, "we got a fair-sized rapids coming this very afternoon."

"You mean Dead Man's Rapids?" Nevers asked.

"That's the one."

For the next hour the river meandered through a big swamp. Ben admired the pale-green needles on the tamaracks. And he and Nevers watched a pair of turtles sleeping on a gray rock.

"Keep slogging," Mike waved to two of his crew who were clearing logs off a muddy hummock near the shore.

Soon the hills got steeper on both sides of the river, and the timber changed to a mix of red and white pine.

When the current began to speed up, Ben heard a familiar sound. "Rapids ahead?"

Mike nodded. "Get ready for a sleigh ride."

Ben glanced at Nevers. Now that they were approaching the famous rapids, Ben suddenly felt nervous.

"You want to get out and walk?" Mike grinned.

"And miss the ride?" Ben pretended not to be scared.

"You favoring the right side, Sard?" Mike called.

"Ya," Sard replied, as the noise of the rapids got louder.

Mike looked at Ben and Nevers. "You aren't gonna pass up a front-deck view, are you?"

"Course not," Ben said, though he wasn't sure he wanted a close look at Dead Man's Rapids.

When Ben reached the front deck, he could see the approach to this rapids was different than any they'd yet seen. A mossy cliff rose to the left, and a rock ledge stood on the right. And between them the dark water fell straight out of sight.

"Hang on, ladies," Sard called, laughing when he saw the boys were already clutching the door frame.

When the wanigan hit the rapids, it dropped straight down. Ben felt his stomach jump into his throat as the boat tilted forward. A loud crack shook the bow, and a pile of tin dishes clattered to the floor. Nevers yelled, but the thundering water drowned him out. Mike steered the wanigan so close to the rock ledge that Ben could have touched the pale lichens.

As the wanigan sped faster, the floorboards vibrated under Ben's boots, and water sprayed his face. Sard spread his legs to brace himself and held the bow oar up and ready. Ben couldn't understand why Sard was even bothering to steer, when he looked downriver and saw a sharp bend.

The free fall of the wanigan stopped when it hit the flat at the base of the rapids. Ben and Nevers both crashed to their knees, and water washed over the bow, drenching their pants.

The bow jumped back up, and the wanigan veered straight for the cliff! Sard pulled on his oar and hollered, "Hang tight," fighting to turn the boat. They swept past the cliff, just missing a jagged point of rock.

A moment later the white-water run was over. The wanigan floated into a still pool. And the roar of the rapids began to fade.

Ben stared at Nevers's sopping hair and his wide eyes. "You look like a drowned rat."

"Speak for yourself."

Ben looked down. His shirt and pants were soaked, and his hair was dripping onto his boots.

Sard grinned at them. "Vat did you think of your first real rapids, girls?"

Too stunned to reply, Ben wiped his face with his shirtsleeve.

"Anything get busted?" Mike asked.

"We made out fine," Sard said. Then he looked toward the hummingbird nest. "Did our little friend ride the rapids?"

"She sat tight the whole way," Mike said.

Just then Mac, who was waiting onshore, said, "I see our cookees got their official Blackwater River baptism."

After they tied up the wanigan, Ben pointed downstream. "That's strange."

A pair of moss-covered calk boots hung from a maple branch that stuck out over the river.

"Why would anybody leave a pair of boots?" Nevers asked.

"By the look of that cracked leather, they've been hanging awhile."

"Four years to be exact."

Ben turned. It was Mike. "How do you know?"

"I was here. Nate Wilken was the fella's name. He'd been driving logs his whole life. But a turn of bad luck sent him down that round river we'll all ride one day."

"Round river?" Nevers asked.

"The river of eternity," Mike said.

When Nevers still looked confused, Sard called through the door. "It means *tot*, you dummkopf. Dead."

"It happened right past that tree." Mike pointed. "Nate was riding a log and whistling like he always did. He bumped a rock and pitched into the river. We didn't think nothing of it. We all take spills. But just like that," Mike snapped his fingers, "the logs closed over him. Everybody scrambled to help, but he never came up. We found his body a half mile downstream."

Mike paused as the boots swung in the breeze. "I'd better go see how my crew is doing back in that bog."

As Mike walked off, Ben thought about the dead lumberjack they'd seen at the start of the trip. He still couldn't get the picture out of his mind: the pale, bloated face, the hand waving in the current, the eyes staring toward something unknown.

"Imagine the horror of getting pushed underwater like that!" Ben said.

Nevers nodded. "You'd fight for breath. But the logs would beat you down again and again."

Ben and Nevers stared into the black water.

"'The rest is silence.'" A voice spoke above them.

Sard was leaning over the deck railing.

"What's that?" Ben asked.

"'The rest is silence.' It's from a play called *Hamlet*," Sard said. "Dying is a hard thing to figure out, but nobody comes closer to explaining it, and most everything else, than Shakespeare."

"Shakespeare wrote plays, didn't he?" Nevers asked.

"He wrote a whole bushel basketful, Snicklefritz. But it's time you and your partner stop being all sad faced and fetch me some water."

19

Blood and Iron

"Go AHEAD and do it," Nevers said.

"You ask him."

"No, you."

All morning long Ben and Nevers had been trying to talk each other into asking Sard about the knife under his bunk.

After Ben filled the hummingbirds' dish, he said, "Let's draw sticks. The fella who gets the short one has to ask him."

"Ask vat?" The voice made them jump. Sard had come back sooner than they'd expected.

"Ah . . ." Nevers hesitated. "We were just—"

"Go on," Sard said. "Vat were you jawing about?"

"We were just curious," Ben said.

"Spit it out."

"You know that knife of yours?"

"We got lots of knives."

"He means the big one under your bunk," Nevers said.

"That ain't a knife." Sard knelt beside his bunk and pulled out a long, metal scabbard. "It's an army-issue bayonet. I keep it ready at night, just in case." He drew out the shiny blade. "Mean looking, ain't it?" Sard swung the point past Nevers's nose. Then he handed it to Ben. "Feel the heft."

Ben touched the deadly-looking saw teeth on top of the blade.

"Careful. Those work better than a blood gutter."

"What's a blood gutter?" Nevers asked.

"It tears up your guts," Sard smiled. "One twist in your belly, and you won't feel like eating sausage."

Ben felt his stomach twinge.

"Where'd you get a bayonet?" Ben asked.

"Same place I got this," Sard touched his eye patch. "In the war. My own gun blew up in my face."

Ben shivered as he recalled the burnt, wrinkled skin that he'd seen under Sard's eye patch.

"Which war was it?" Nevers asked.

"I was in two wars back in Germany, thanks to Bismarck—they called him 'Blood and Iron' for good reason. When the first war started, I was in college. I didn't think they'd take a science major, but they handed me a Dreyse rifle and marched me into Denmark."

"Didn't they train you none?" Nevers asked.

"They taught me how to pull the trigger. That was it. The Danish war lasted six months, and I went back to school. Two years later, Germany invaded Austria. That was only a seven-week war, but it cost me this eye. "I hit the books again. But just before graduation, we attacked France. That's when I left."

"They wouldna made you fight with one eye," Nevers said.

"I wasn't taking any chances."

"Did you go to college once you got here?" Ben asked.

"I snuck into the U.S. through Canada. Without papers all you can do is knock around the woods. I thought about applying for citizenship, but with America picking fights in Cuba and the Philippines, I wasn't about to get fitted for another uniform."

Sard paused. Ben wondered if he was thinking about the battle that had cost him his eye. Now that he knew Sard had been to college his fancy quotes made sense.

Finally Sard said, "But that's all water under the bridge. You boys better get cooking. Mike'll want his grub soon."

Later, when they were alone, Ben asked, "Did you hear what Sard said?"

"He said a lot."

"Just now. He called us boys instead of dummkopfs or dunderheads."

"Or Snicklefritz," Nevers smiled.

"It almost feels like we got promoted."

All week long Mike had been telling Ben and Nevers about a country store—one of only two stores that lay between Blackwater and the Canadian border. Ben was expecting something like the general store back home, but when Mike steered the wanigan into shore, Ben saw only a small log cabin, along with a half-dozen farmers, who'd turned out to watch the log drive.

Above the front door of the store was a huge sign:

Esko's Emporium
Esko Savela, Jr., Proprietor
Dry Goods and Mercantile

"What's an emporium?" Nevers asked.

Mike said, "A fancy store like you'd find in Chicago or New York City."

"Well, they sure got that wrong."

"It's just like a storekeeper to put on airs," Sard said. "I'd rather muck out a stable than sell potatoes to a bunch of prune-faced farmers."

Next to the store stood a crooked pole with three arrow-shaped signs pointing in different directions and labeled "Marquette, Michigan, 404 miles"; "Astoria, Oregon, 1,831 miles"; and "Helsinki, Finland, 5,062 miles."

"Somebody sure likes signs," Nevers said.

Mike and Ben were still tying the mooring ropes when a lean, rawboned man with white-blond hair came down the bank. "I'm Esko Savela," he said, standing even straighter than Mac, while the rest of the unsmiling folks on shore hung back.

"Welcome to my emporium," Esko said, offering no handshake as he led the way up to his store.

Built of dovetailed logs, Esko's store was smaller than their wanigan. And despite its fancy name, it was mainly empty.

"Have you got any eggs?" Sard asked.

"Not today," Esko said.

"Cinnamon?" Sard asked.

"Only cardamom."

"Then we'll take five cans of lard, a keg of sugar, three sacks of potatoes, and a slab of bacon," Sard said.

"Do you need flour?"

"Any chance you got rye?"

"It's the only kind us Finns use," Esko almost smiled.

Mike's face fell. "Sometimes a fella's luck goes south."

"What's that?" Esko asked.

"Mike ain't a big fan of rye," Sard said.

Esko said, "Once you get used to rye bread, it'll grow on you, and you won't want anything else."

"Well it ain't growed on me yet," Mike said.

Sard grinned as Ben and Nevers hauled the supplies to the wanigan. "I always heard that Finlanders favored black bread. I wonder if they have a taste for sauerkraut, too."

Mike shook his head. "Eating black bread is bad enough. I never understood folks calling rotten cabbage food."

20

A Wassel Tale

EACH EVENING the fellas came back cold and wet but full of energy. The men used the dishing-up line as much for teasing as for filling their plates. And when they sat by the campfire to eat, they swapped stories between bitefuls of beans.

One night as Ben carried the coffeepot up, Nevers said, "I'm wore out from just feeding these fellas. But they're still feisty after wrestling logs all day."

When Dynamite Dick saw the coffeepot coming, he spit into the fire and asked Jimmy, "With this late spring you think we might have a snow wassel lurking in the brush?"

"I wouldn't doubt there's one or two around," Jimmy said.

"What's a snow wassel?" Nevers asked.

At the logging camp last winter Ben had heard lots of tales about north-woods creatures, but a snow wassel was new to him.

Jimmy said, "Wassels are legless, snaky-looking critters as long as a bear. In the winter they burrow under the snow."

Dick nodded as he stared into the fire. "And they're meaner than wolverines."

Jimmy continued. "Wassels eat four times every day, just like us river pigs. Their favorite meal is timber wolves. After wintering here in Minnesota, come spring they grow out legs and travel to the Canadian barrens, where they hibernate all summer."

"So they're gone now?" Nevers's eyes were big.

"There may be a few patches of snow left in the swamps, which means—" Dick's voice slowed even more than normal, and he peered off into the darkness.

"Which means what?" Nevers asked.

"Which means we'd better take care. 'Cause there's one food that wassels love to snack on in the spring." Dick waved Ben closer and held out his cup for a refill.

"What food might that be?" Nevers asked.

Ben had never heard Dick talk so long at one stretch, but he kept going. "When the pickings are slim, and the wolves few and far between, a wassel hunts by crouching in the brush beside the river. He waits real patient." Dick took a sip of coffee. "Then when a wanigan floats by—" Dick suddenly sped up. "Quick as a blink that wassel snatches a boy off the deck and chews him up."

Just as Dick said, "snatches a boy," Jimmy's hand shot out and grabbed Nevers's ankle.

"Yeow!" Nevers yelled, jumping into the air and stumbling backward. Luckily, Mike caught him by the arm and kept him from falling into the fire.

The fellas couldn't stop laughing.

Nevers said, "I knowed you all were joshing," which made everyone laugh even more.

Later the talk shifted to the river pigs' favorite subject other than food and women: past river drives. The fellas constantly compared their current drive with former drives. They discussed the quantity of the logs, the water levels, and their progress. But most of all they loved to talk logjams.

Jimmy was the logjam expert. "As I youngster I saw some big jams on the Penobscot, but the worst I ever faced was on the St. Croix at Angel Rock. It was June of '86. A hundred and fifty million feet of prime pine got hung up. Two hundred men picked away for six weeks, but we couldn't bust her loose. The company brought in two Mississippi River steamboats and a hundred horses, but nothing helped."

"They finally planted twenty-four pounds of dynamite." Dick whistled softly. "That wicked little firecracker blew logs a hundred feet into the air and sent an avalanche of timber downriver, but nobody got hurt. It took seventy men working into September to clean up the rear."

After Jimmy finished his story, some of the fellas mentioned famous jams in other places, like the Mississippi, Wolf River, and the Chippewa, but Dick said, "Let's not forget the Blackwater can jam up pretty good, too."

Mike nodded. "All it takes is one log hanging up in the wrong place."

"And we can't count on steamboats and horses to help us out," Mac said.

Later, after the boys had climbed into their bunks, Sard held up his bayonet and said, "Hey Snicklefritz, you care to sleep with this tonight?"

"Why would I want a knife in bed?"

"To protect yourself in case a snow wassel climbs on board." Sard was still cackling after he'd lain down.

Ben was usually too tired to dream, but he imagined a huge logjam in his sleep. A high wall of logs had choked the Blackwater to a trickle. Ben stood below the jam holding a pike pole. Water dripped off the end of a log and onto his boots.

"Pull the key log!" a man called. "It's right in front of you." Ben looked up at the cross-piled logs.

"Pull!" the voice shouted.

Ben turned to look. Sard stood grinning in his greasy apron.

Just then Ben heard a rumbling. He felt the river rock tremble under his boots. At that same moment the drip of water above him turned to a spout. When he looked up, the whole wall of logs was falling toward him.

"Run, you dummkopf!" Sard hollered.

"Run," Ben sat up in bed shouting. "Run, run . . ."

Ben opened his eyes. Nevers was patting his shoulder. "Take it easy," Nevers said. "It was just a bad dream."

Ben's heart hammered in his chest. "Sorry," Ben said. "But it seemed so real."

Sard laughed. "Does Little Ben have monsters chasing him?"

"Go back to sleep," Ben said.

"Thanks for the entertainment," Sard chuckled.

21

A Hand in the Bush

"HELP, BEN!" Nevers called from the brush above the river. "I forgot the toilet paper."

Ben stepped into the wanigan and reached for the Sears catalog that was hanging by the back door. Then he remembered the trick that Nevers had played on him at the beginning of the trip.

Ben stepped outside.

"What's taking so long?" Nevers called.

"Use some leaves like the other fellas do," Ben said.

"Bennn . . . !"

"Or should I tear a piece of burlap off a potato sack?"

Ben smiled when Nevers didn't say anything more.

Ben forgot all about the joke until the following evening when he and Nevers were washing up on the back deck. "My fingers feel funny," Nevers said, holding out his right hand.

"It's too dark to see. Let's look at it inside."

Under the lantern light Ben saw that Nevers's palm and fingers were red and puffy. "It itches something powerful," Nevers said, digging at the skin with his fingers. And I feel like I got ants in my pants."

Sard peered at Nevers's hand. "That's an ugly rash. If I didn't know better, I'd say you'd been playing in poison ivy."

"Where would I ever—" Nevers stopped. "What about those leaves I used up in the bushes yesterday?"

"Let's hope that's not it," Ben said.

"If your pants are itching, you'd better drop your drawers and let me have a look," Sard said.

"I ain't takin' off my pants," Nevers said.

"I can't help what I can't see." Sard took the lantern off the hook and set it on the floor. "Let's see what you got."

Nevers stood with his feet planted.

"Get on with it," Sard said. "It's past my bedtime."

Nevers dug at his palm. "If I weren't itching so doggone bad, I wouldn't be doing this." He turned and unbuttoned his pants.

Feeling bad, Ben looked away as his friend dropped his pants.

Sard started laughing.

"What is it?" Nevers looked over his shoulder.

"You got a rash on your rear the exact size of your hand. I can see the outline of your fingers clear as day."

"So I gave myself poison ivy?" Nevers glared at Ben.

"And a healthy dose of it at that," Sard said.

"How can I stop the itching?" Nevers clenched his teeth.

"First you gotta rinse out your clothes to make sure there's no poison left on 'em. Then wash your skin with soap and water as hot as you can stand."

"Will that fix it?" Nevers asked.

"It'll help, but there's no cure for poison ivy. It'll get worse before it gets better."

Ben looked at Nevers. "I'm real sorry. I never meant—"

"Who'da thought there was poison ivy in that brush? And you did owe me for tossing you that scrap of burlap."

"I don't care who caused what," Sard said. "I'm hitting the sack." He crawled into his bunk and called, "Sweet dreams, nimrods," before he started snoring.

Ben heated some water and washed out Nevers's clothes, while Nevers sat in a bucket of hot, soapy water.

After Ben hung Nevers's clothes beside the stove to dry, the boys climbed into their bunks. "Did the soap help?" Ben asked.

"I woulda said yes five minutes ago, but the more my skin dries out, the itchier it gets."

"Maybe it'll be better tomorrow," Ben said. But he could already hear Nevers turning over and gritting his teeth as he tried not to dig at his rash.

Later Ben woke to the sound of footsteps. The back door was open, and Nevers was pacing across the deck.

Ben stepped outside. "Is it worse?"

"It feels like somebody scratched my skin with sandpaper and sprinkled pepper on top of it." Nevers held out his swollen hand. "The more I scratch, the worse it itches. But I can't stop."

Ben was about tell Nevers how sorry he was again, when Sard yelled, "Get to bed, you blockheads."

Over the next few days Nevers's rash got worse. Everybody in the crew recommended a different cure. And Nevers was so desperate he tried every single one.

One morning Dick told Nevers to coat his rash with lard. Nevers smeared himself up after the fellas left. And he seemed better at first. Then he started itching so bad that he ran up the bank pants-less and scratched his rear against a popple tree, whimpering "Ow, ow, ow," the whole time. After yelling for Ben to heat some water, he sat in a soapy bucket to ease the pain.

The next day Jimmy said that airing out his rash was the only thing that would help. So Nevers walked around all morning with the back flap of his long underwear hanging open.

Sard teased Nevers, claiming that he deserved bonus pay if his cookee was gonna "parade around with a bare hinder." But all Nevers got out of his "airing" was a couple of splinters in his butt when he accidentally brushed against the deck railing.

"I think you just gotta give it time to go away," Ben said.

"Easy for you to say," Nevers said, showing Ben the puffy red blisters on his palm that were now oozing clear liquid.

The only thing that kept Nevers's mind off his misery was staying busy, but his sore hand made some jobs impossible. That meant Ben had to do all the two-handed work like peeling potatoes, slicing bread, and chopping wood. The one chore Nevers looked forward to was dishwashing, because the sudsy water made his hand feel better, even if it was only for a short while.

Altogether the crew recommended a half-dozen cures to Nevers, including pasting himself with everything from baking soda and cooked oatmeal to raw potato slices and brown paper soaked in vinegar. But nothing helped.

Sard laughed every time Nevers tried something new, saying, "Mac might have to dock your pay if you keep plastering our cooking supplies on your fanny."

I Wish I May, I Wish I Might

"FEEL THAT AIR?" Nevers asked.

Ben was lying in bed, half asleep, trying to block out Sard's awful singing.

"What about it?" Ben yawned.

Nevers was standing in the doorway, grinning. "We finally got us a Carolina spring morning." Nevers's rash had faded, and he was in much better spirits.

Ben joined Nevers. A warm breeze drifted off the water. The birds were chattering in the treetops, and a pair of mallards were quacking and scouring the river bottom for food.

"Even the ducks look happy," Ben said.

For the first lunch they parked the wanigan near another homestead. The cabin was a converted trapper's shack roofed with moss-covered sheets of birch bark, and the building looked ready to collapse. The family had two babies and owned one milk cow, which had its ribs showing.

Sard introduced himself and said, "I'd like to buy some eggs and buttermilk if you've got some to spare."

Instead of haggling like he did last time, Sard paid the farmer his price. On their way back to the wanigan, Nevers asked, "Did you give those folks extra money because they was so poor?"

"We needed eggs," Sard said. "Besides money's like manure."

"How's that?" Ben asked.

"It don't do no good unless you spread it around. Ha, ha, ha."

When the boys walked on the back deck, Mike was smiling. "Seeing that bony old cow over there reminded me of a riddle."

"What is that?" Nevers asked.

"Why does a milk stool have only three legs?"

"Don't know," Nevers said.

"'Cause the cow's got the udder." Mike and Sard both cackled a long time over that one.

"Now we got two of 'em carrying on," Ben said.

By midafternoon the sun was full on the back deck, and Nevers said, "It's hotter than a billy goat in a pepper patch."

"I wish it would cool down," Ben said.

"Didn't I warn you about wishing?"

"No way is my wishing gonna change the weather."

"I just hope you don't wish us up a bunch of trouble."

The heat continued for one more day. But on the following morning the wind swung into the north.

"Look over yonder," Nevers said to Ben, pointing to some dark clouds. "See what you gone and done."

"Don't blame me. I wished for that cooldown two days ago."

"That's a mackerel sky if I ever saw one," Jimmy said.

"Mackerel?" Nevers asked.

"See how it's all streaked with gray? We got a saying in Maine: A mackerel sky means two days wet and one day dry."

True to Jimmy's prediction, a light rain started that morning. By dinnertime it was pouring so hard that putting up the tents and fetching the balsam boughs left Ben and Nevers a muddy mess. And there was no way to get a campfire started.

"No sense stringing up a clothesline," Sard said. "The fellas will just have to sleep in their clothes."

The men ate standing up under the trees and shoveled their food down even faster than usual. Mike grinned when his plate filled up with rain. "We got us a real bean floater tonight."

Everyone laughed but Klondike, who groused, "I'd rather be back in Alaska than on this swamp of a river."

"If Alaska's so great," Dick said, "Why don't you jump in the water and swim back up there?"

Slim changed the subject, saying, "We'll be working the wings tomorrow."

"What's that mean?" Nevers asked.

"A rising river floats the logs toward the banks, and they get hung up on everything. It's easier to run logs when the water's falling because they center.

"Looks like Old Sard is working the wings already," Mac pointed down the bank.

Sard was kneeling in the mud beside the river, while a mother woodchuck ran in circles above him. Water was sloshing into the woodchuck's den, and Sard was handing her babies up to her.

Jimmy shook his head. "I never thought I'd see that ornery old sausage boiler mothering woodchucks!"

"If only he put that much effort into cooking," Mike said.

Later, Nevers asked Sard, "Why'd you bother to save those varmints?"

"Those critters needed my help," Sard said. "I learned a long time ago if you help an animal, it's grateful. A famous fella once said that the main difference between a dog and a man is if you help a starving dog, it won't bite you."

"I can't argue that," Nevers said.

Later, while the boys were washing the dishes, Nevers asked Ben, "You ready to admit what you done?"

"Don't start in on my wishing. Rain comes from the clouds, not from somebody hoping for it."

"I heard you wish. And look what's happened," Nevers said.

"Watch this then," Ben said, holding up both his hands. "Rain, rain, go away." He paused. "You see anything happen?"

"This ain't something to joke about."

"There is one bright spot to all this rain," Ben said.

"And what might that be?"

Ben held up a dripping plate. "They come prerinsed."

But Nevers wouldn't smile.

By the time the boys were ready for bed, the rain on the tarpaper roof had changed to sharp little ticks. "You reckon that's sleet?" Nevers asked.

Ben slid open the back door. "The deck's already icing up."

"Shut that door!" Sard hollered.

After the boys climbed into their bunks, the noise on the roof quieted. "It's about time," Nevers said. "I was getting a headache from that rattling."

The next morning Ben woke up to a cool breeze. Sard was standing in the doorway. "That sleet changed to snow."

"Not in May!" Ben said. He felt the cold through his wool socks as he padded to the door. Ten inches of wet snow had blanketed the back deck and railings. The tree branches and the tent roofs sagged under the weight.

"Welcome to Minnesnowta," Sard laughed. Then he looked at the hummingbird nest. "Our little gal made it through the night, but we'd better warm her some sugar water."

The trees, which had been filled with songbirds yesterday, were silent and white.

Sard pulled off his shirt and kicked some wet snow off the deck. Then he knelt down and splashed water on his bare chest, singing extra loud: "*Du, du liegst mir im Herzen . . .*"

After Sard toweled off, he stepped back inside and sneezed.

"Gesundheit," he blessed himself and pulled out his medicine box. But before he could swallow his first pill, he sneezed again.

"What's the matter?" Nevers teased. "I thought your medicine protected you from every ailment known to man?"

"I'll be fine," Sard said, squinting at his Syrup of Figs bottle. "I just need to up my dose." He took two extra swigs straight from the bottle.

As Ben stoked up the stove, Jimmy and Mike stepped onto the back deck, and Jimmy said, "'Tis a fine—" But he stopped.

Mike looked at Jimmy. "You were saying?"

For a moment Jimmy stared at the deep snow, tongue-tied. Then he smiled. "'Tis a fine bit of fortune the river didn't freeze solid with this chill in the air."

"Chill!" Mike groused. "It's cold enough to freeze an Eskimo."

When it was time to lard up, Klondike whined, "I was hoping we'd get the day off."

Slim looked Klondike in the eye. "There ain't no days off on a log drive. We ride this cork pine 'til the job is done."

The rest of the fellas stripped off their pants and underwear without complaining and smeared themselves up with lard, as if it were perfectly normal to drive logs after a snowstorm.

As Ben and Nevers were finishing up the breakfast dishes, Ben heard a gurgling noise. He looked at Nevers. "Was that you?"

Nevers shook his head.

The gurgling came again, louder. The boys looked at Sard.

His lips were tight, and he was hunched over, clutching his belly.

"You okay?" Ben asked.

Sard frowned. "I mighta overdosed myself with that fig syrup. My gut don't feel so—" Sard stopped, and still bent over, he hightailed it out the door.

Ben and Nevers couldn't help laughing.

"It ain't nice of us to laugh," Nevers said.

"I know," Ben said. "But as contrary as Sard is, I'm thinking a case of diarrhea might improve his disposition."

And they both laughed even harder.

Despite the snow and the cold, Sard had to run outside and go to the bathroom a half-dozen times that morning. Each time he came back looking a little paler.

Finally he asked, "Suppose you boys can handle the lunch? I think I need a lay down."

With that, Sard crashed on his bunk, and a few minutes later he was snoring.

While Sard was out of commission, Ben and Nevers surprised Mike's crew with some fresh biscuits at the first lunch. They waited until Mike was ready to dish up. Then Ben opened the oven door and pulled out a pan of still-warm biscuits.

Mike stared for a moment. Then he held out his hand and said, "Somebody pinch me quick! Prove I ain't dreaming."

One Shoe Off and One Shoe On

THE NEXT MORNING Sard's stomach was better, but when he stepped outside to take his bath, he coughed and sneezed. He splashed water on his head and tried singing, but he coughed so much that he had to stop.

"Sounds like he's gonna choke to death," Ben said.

Sard hacked and spit into the water. Then he blew his nose farmer style, holding one nostril shut and spewing green snot into the river.

"That man is a human pig," Ben said.

"I'm gonna throw up," Nevers said, turning away as Sard cleared his second nostril and rubbed his hands together.

"I never shoulda wished my pa away."

"About time you admitted it." Nevers was still gagging.

Sard came back inside and took all his medicine except for his Syrup of Figs. Ben asked, "I thought that syrup kept you from getting sick?"

"I woulda been twice as bad if I hadn't dosed myself. Besides"—Sard paused for a hacking cough—"I got a special cure that'll pull me through."

Sard took a cup of hot water and stirred in a tablespoon of honey. Then he got out the kerosene can.

114

"That's poison!" Ben said.

"I ain't gonna swallow it." He added a splash of kerosene to his cup. "It's my gargling formula."

Ben stared as Sard stepped outside, gargled the oily mixture, and spit it into the river.

Nevers said, "We'd better not light any matches around him."

Sard walked back inside and belched. Stinking of kerosene, he sat down and took off one boot and sock. He laid his dirty sock flat on the table like he was going to iron it.

"What you aiming to do?" Nevers asked.

Ignoring Nevers, Sard sliced off a piece of raw bacon, peppered it, and shoved it inside his sock.

"You reckon he's gonna eat a sock now?" Nevers asked Ben.

Still not talking, Sard tied the sock around his neck.

"A poultice?" Ben asked.

"I seen lots of poultices—they favored mustard and onions at my orphanage—but I never heard of pork and pepper."

"It fixes my cold every time," Sard said.

When the fellas came in for breakfast, they gave Sard some strange looks. Since he didn't have a spare sock, he served breakfast with only one boot on.

Mac stared at the sock around Sard's throat. "Is this some new German-style fashion?"

Everyone laughed. Then Jimmy asked Sard, "Ain't you afraid you're gonna walk in circles with only one boot on?"

By the next morning nearly all the snow had melted, and Ben was glad to wake to songbirds again. He'd worried that the birds wouldn't survive the storm.

Just then a horrible sound came from the back deck.

"Are you hearing what I am?" Nevers groaned from his bunk.

"Sard's gotta be too sick to be up this early," Ben said. But when he looked out the door, Sard was splashing water on his bald head and singing louder than ever.

Grinning, Sard walked inside drying his hairy chest. He wasn't coughing, and his eyes looked bright.

"What happened to your cold?" Ben asked.

"I'm cured," Sard said. "Not so much as a tickle." He pointed to his neck, which was no longer wrapped in the dirty sock. "My poultice did the trick."

24

Dick Goes Fishing

THE FELLAS were getting so tired of Sard's cooking that more of them joined Mike in reminiscing about past meals. Slim even waxed sentimental one evening about Pa's cookies. He tapped his pipe on a log and said, "Remember those melt-in-your-mouth sugar cookies Jack used to bake on Sundays?"

"Would you all stop it!" Dynamite Dick startled everyone by talking twice as fast as normal. "We're hungry enough to chaw the bark off a popple tree, but it don't help none going on about food we ain't never getting on this drive."

"You won't hear me complaining as long as I got my beans and my bread," Jimmy said, wiping his plate with a piece of Sard's rye. "Though," he banged the crust on his tin plate, "this is a might heavy for my taste."

"That bread would work for a boat anchor," Mike said.

The fellas laughed, but they were quieter than usual as they finished their coffee and crawled into the tents.

The following afternoon a charge of dynamite went off downriver.

"Dick will be all smiles tonight," Ben said.

Nevers nodded. "Nothing cheers him up more than blasting things to pieces."

When the sacking crew came back for their second lunch, Mike led the way. As the men got closer, Ben could see that Mike was carrying a short loop of rope with four northerns strung on it.

"Dick stunned a few fish and figured you might want to fry 'em up for supper," Mike said.

"I've been hankering for fried fish and taters," Nevers said. When Ben offered to clean the fish, Sard said, "I'll take care of 'em."

After the boys set up tents and went back to the wanigan, Ben expected to see pan-ready fish fillets. "Where's the fish?"

"It don't take long to saw up a few fish," Sard said.

"But the frying pan's empty," Nevers said.

"But the pot ain't," Sard pointed at the iron kettle.

Ben walked over to the bubbling kettle. He'd been looking forward to crispy, fresh-fried fillets. Ben lifted the lid, while Nevers peered over his shoulder.

"It's fish stew." Ben said, staring at the white chunks of chopped fish and potatoes floating along with the fish heads.

"You're cooking the heads, too?" Nevers asked.

Ben felt queasy as he stared at a glassy eyeball.

"The heads give it flavor," Sard said. "A Finlander from Michigan taught me the recipe. It slides down real easy."

When the crews got back that evening, Mike clapped Dick on the shoulder and said, "Good job fishing today."

"I might give up on using a fishing pole," Dick grinned, showing his brown teeth.

"It's been a long time since I've had a good mess of fish," Klondike said. "Though I am partial to salmon."

As usual, Mike was the first one in the line, but he waved Dick ahead, saying, "You authored this feast."

Dick and Mike were grinning broad enough to break their faces as they marched inside. "Where's the fish?" Dick asked.

Ben pointed at the kettle.

When Dick lifted the lid, Ben expected him to yell or swear, but he just looked confused.

Mike looked over Dick's shoulder and blinked as if he wasn't sure his eyes were working. Finally he said, "There's your fish. Old One Pot has gone and done it again."

Dick nodded. "Fish soup with the heads and all."

"Ain't you ever seen soup?" Sard asked. "Get dished up before the other fellas trample you down."

As news of the fish soup spread down the line, the fellas suddenly got quiet.

It wasn't until later when Ben and Nevers carried up the coffeepot and cookies that the mood lightened.

Mike saw the boys coming and said, "Dessert's on the way. What do you suppose it'll be? Fish cakes?"

With that, everyone had a good laugh.

25

The Key Log

BEN WOKE with a start. Something had jarred his bunk. He listened, but everything was quiet. Just as he was about go back to sleep, something bumped the wanigan again.

"You feel that?" Ben asked, but Nevers was asleep.

Ben climbed down and stepped onto the back deck. The air smelled damp and piney. Since there was a light breeze, Ben thought the bateau might be banging into the hull. But the river was oddly silent. When Ben peered downstream, the clouds opened for a moment and starlight shined down. He saw that the whole river was filled with logs. And not one was moving!

"Nevers! Sard! Wake up! We got a jam." Then Ben ran up to the tents, knowing that a logjam could put the whole drive at risk. It could flood the land for miles upriver. Or worse, the water could cut a new channel and leave their logs high and dry.

Mac and Dick were the first ones up. Mac said, "It's probably that narrows we were worried about."

"I'll grab a few sticks of dynamite," Dick said, as the other fellas began to crawl out of the tents.

Mac glanced at the sky. "We won't have enough light to work for an hour, but we can set up." Mac turned to Mike: "Get a coil of rope and a couple lanterns, and make sure the fellas bring their peaveys and cant hooks."

Ben and Nevers followed the men through the woods. But Mike's lantern was so far ahead that they stumbled a lot. Once Ben got slapped by a branch and fell backwards.

"Don't be laying down on the job back there," Jimmy called.

When they reached the jam, the ten-foot-high pile of crisscrossed logs looked like an angry giant had flung them down. The air stunk like a swamp. And Ben heard a tiny trickle of water.

Mac studied the tangle of logs, and he noted the water flowing around the jam on the far bank, which was a bad sign.

"We'd better move fast before we lose our head of water."

"Want me to blast her?" Dick sounded hopeful.

"We don't want to turn good timber into toothpicks just yet."

"There's gotta be a key log," Jimmy said.

Mac nodded. "But let's be careful."

The men fanned out across the face of the jam. Ben reached for a peavey, but Mac said, "No, son. You and your partner make sure that rope ain't kinked or knotted. We may need it directly."

While Ben and Nevers checked the rope, the men in the muddy riverbed used peaveys and cant hooks to pry loose logs. For once no one joked. And everyone kept an eye on the pile above him.

Mac directed the fellas from the shore, calling, "Watch that stick to your left, Dick," or "Take her easy now, Jimmy."

Each time a log clattered onto the wet rocks, the sound startled Ben. And the fellas all turned to make sure that the whole jam wasn't breaking loose.

Klondike was the only man who hung back. Ben could tell he was staying close to shore to avoid danger.

As the sun rose, Ben could see that more water was flowing around the far side of the jam.

Mac spoke to Ben and Nevers without taking his eyes off the logs. "Make sure you clear out of the way if she busts loose. Everybody'll be hightailing it to shore."

The men picked at the logs until well after sunrise, but they only managed to start one little spurt of water. Suddenly Mac said, "That's it. Come on in."

The fellas slogged to shore with smelly black mud smeared on their pants. "Time to blast?" Dick asked.

But Jimmy said, "Give me a few more minutes."

"I don't like the looks of it," Mac said.

"I know I can get her."

Mac paced down the shore and stared at the jam for a full minute. When he came back, he said, "We'd have to rope you up."

"Let's do it," Jimmy said, raising his arms so Mike could cinch a loop around his chest.

Mac said, "Three or four of you feed out the rope and be ready to pull."

Mike and two of the strongest fellas picked up the rope.

Holding just a cant hook, Jimmy walked into the riverbed, while the men on shore played out the rope. Mike held the rope shoulder high so the coils couldn't snag on any rocks.

Once Jimmy reached the center of the jam, Mac called, "Ten minutes is all you get. Then we'll turn Dick loose."

Ben was nervous as he watched Jimmy pull on one log and then another. "Watch yourself," Mac called from shore.

"I think I see the key log," Jimmy said. He clamped his cant hook on the end of a log that was sticking out at a funny angle, and he lifted with all his strength. But it wouldn't budge. "She's wicked tight." Jimmy grunted and tried again.

Mac looked at Mike and raised his arm. "Take the slack out of that line."

Jimmy bent his knees and lifted hard with his legs and back. When the log popped free, Mac was about to drop his arm and yell, "Pull." But the log splashed into a puddle at Jimmy's feet, and the jam never shifted.

"Dang it," Mike said, and the shoulders of the fellas sagged.

Suddenly a spout of water gushed out, knocking Jimmy backwards.

"Pull!" Mac yelled. "Pull! Pull!"

Mike pulled the rope hand over hand, while the men behind him gathered up the slack.

As the wall of logs and water tumbled down where Jimmy had been standing, Ben closed his eyes. Jimmy was a goner for sure.

That's when Mac yelled, "Clear out! The wing's sliding!"

"Lordy!" Nevers eyes opened wide as the logs on the side of the jam surged toward them.

"Move!" Mac shouted as everyone stumbled up the bank.

Mike kept pulling the rope as fast as he could, but Jimmy was nowhere in sight.

Ben had given up hope, when Jimmy's head finally popped out of the foam near shore. In one movement, Mike grabbed the loop around Jimmy's chest and dragged him up the bank just as the logs thundered past.

Jimmy lay flat on his back with his eyes closed. Mike knelt down, saying, "I'll roll him over in case he took in water."

But when Mike reached out, Jimmy's eyes flicked open, and he pushed Mike's hand away. "You've tossed me around enough for one day." Jimmy sat up and spit out a mouthful of brown water.

Mike grinned. "I was afraid we'd have to tell that pretty, young wife of yours that you'd headed down the round river."

"I wouldn't worry about her," Jimmy said. "She could replace my old carcass with a new model any day."

The men all laughed.

"But she'd never find a tougher bean eater than you," Mac said.

26

Devil Mouse

THE NEXT MORNING Ben was lying in bed trying not to listen to Sard singing on the back deck. Suddenly Sard yelled, "*Teufel Maus*," and stomped his foot so hard that the whole wanigan shook.

Sard came through the door mumbling, "Another devil mouse." Ben was about to tease Sard, when he saw his hands were shaking.

"You okay?" Ben asked.

"It didn't sneak in here did it?" Sard scanned the room.

"So why do you call mice devils?" Nevers asked.

Sard looked like he was about to say something sarcastic, but his face turned serious. "It dates back to that war I told you about." Sard stopped and toweled off his bald head, as if he weren't going to say anything more. But then he went on.

"Mice never bothered me until we reached the front. There'd been a skirmish the week before, and my unit had to march past a pile of dead soldiers. Seeing the bloated bodies, some no older than you runts, woulda been shock enough. But when I saw the mice and rats crawling over their faces, it rattled me good."

Nevers looked ready to gag, but Sard only grinned. "Sorry you asked now, Snicklefritz? I'll spare you the details. But let's just say those devil mice like to eat the eyeballs first. How's that for fine hors d'oeuvres? Ha, ha, ha."

Sard kept laughing as he stepped outside to hang up his towel.

Ben felt sick to his stomach. He thought back to the dead lumberjack they'd seen in the river. If the sight of one body gave him bad dreams, he could imagine how walking through a battlefield of corpses would mess up a fella's mind. No wonder Sard was such a hard fella.

Only a moment later Sard said, "Would you look at that?"

"What now?" Ben asked. He stepped outside, expecting another gross remark, but Sard smiled and pointed instead. Two tiny hummingbird hatchlings were scrunched down in the nest.

Nevers frowned. "They're shriveled up like little lizards. You reckon they'll make it?"

Just then the mother bird zipped over the roof and chirped, dive-bombing Nevers's head. He squealed and ducked.

Sard laughed. "With all the fight in that momma, those birds should do just fine."

Through the morning the mother hummingbird was a whirlwind of energy. Every few minutes she shared a drink of sugar water with her chicks or brought them back tiny bugs. But if Ben or Nevers got too close, she buzzed past their ears.

When it came time to move the wanigan, Mike was careful with the gangplanks. "We don't want to upset momma," he smiled.

Since there weren't any sharp bends or rapids in this stretch of river, Mike let Ben and Nevers try steering. Though the boys could barely lift the twenty-foot-long oar, Mike showed them how to use their weight for leverage.

"This ain't like turning your baby-sized canoe," Mike said. Then looking at the baby birds, he added, "Too bad those little hummers don't grow a few sizes bigger. If we hitched up a flock of 'em, they could tow us all the way to Canada. Which reminds me of a story. Did I ever tell you about the winter I was driving a tote wagon across a frozen lake, and a pack of wolves chased me down?"

Ben smiled at Nevers, knowing there was no stopping Mike from telling his story.

27

The Sluice Gate

WHEN BEN SAW his first sluice dam, he was impressed by how sturdy it looked. Unlike the crude splash dams that Dick had been blasting, this one had neat wooden cribs on both sides and a chute with a gate in the middle.

To guide the logs through the sluice, the drive crew and sacking crew worked together on the upstream side, steering the logs into the chute. The jam crew spread out below the dam to keep the logs moving after they shot through.

Talking over the roar of the water, Mike asked Ben and Nevers, "You gonna ride the wanigan when we take her through?"

"Will it fit through there?" Ben eyed the chute.

"We'll have six inches to spare on both sides," Mike said.

"That'll take some straight steering," Nevers said.

"What do you say?" Ben asked Nevers.

"I'm fixin' to ride," Nevers smiled.

On the way back to the wanigan, Ben and Nevers practiced log walking. Since the channel was filled from bank to bank, the logs along the shore were locked in tight and easy to balance on.

Ben jumped onto a thick red pine next to the shore.

"Wait for me," Nevers called.

Raising their knees high and enjoying the sound of their

spiked boots biting into the wet bark, the boys ran the length of one log after another, all the way back to the wanigan.

"Look at me," Nevers said, walking on a log that stuck out past the end of the wanigan.

"Careful," Ben said.

"There's nothing to it." Nevers grabbed a broom from the deck to help him balance, and he stepped farther out.

"Watch yourself," Ben called.

When Nevers reached the middle of the river, he said, "Come and try it, Ben! The logs are locked tight together." But as he spoke, the end of his log dipped, and he dropped the broom.

"Nevers!" Ben yelled.

"Dunce," Sard mumbled.

As Nevers waved his arms for balance, his log started moving downstream. He whipped his head from side to side, looking for a route to shore.

"Hang on," Ben hollered, as Nevers's log picked up speed.

Just then a bigger log bumped Nevers from behind, and he lost his footing.

Even before Nevers hit the water, Ben was sprinting toward the dam. "I'll get help!" he yelled.

"Tell 'em he's grabbed ahold of a log," Sard called.

Ben burst out of the woods yelling, "It's Nevers! He fell in. He's floating downstream!"

Mac, who was standing on the near crib, waved to the men. "Be on the lookout. Nevers is coming this way."

Everyone stared upriver. Ben climbed up beside Mac. "Be careful, son."

The fellas kept scanning the water. And as the seconds ticked by, Ben got more nervous. What if the logs had closed over Nevers like they had for that boy back on Dead Man's Rapids?

After what seemed like an hour, Jimmy finally pointed from the far crib, "He's on your side."

Ben got up on his tiptoes to look. Nevers had straddled a log, and he was hanging on for dear life.

"Grab him," Mac yelled.

Nevers smiled when he saw Klondike on a log just a few feet ahead. Nevers leaned forward and reached out.

But instead of bending down and grabbing Nevers's hand like he could have, Klondike froze.

"Get him!" Mac and Jimmy both yelled.

Nevers's eyes were wide with fear as his log sped past the crib and teetered on the brink of the chute. Jimmy reached down with the handle of his pike pole, but it was too late.

Just before the log disappeared into the chute, Nevers laid belly-down and hugged the bark tight.

"Nooo . . ." Ben yelled.

A moment later, Slim, who'd been standing next to Jimmy, let out a curse. Ben turned just in time to see Slim leap from the top of the dam toward the logs below.

Ben held his breath as Slim flew over the roiling water. When Slim landed on a log beside the sluice, his calks drove the log so deep underwater that he got wet to his knees, but he didn't lose his balance. And he didn't lose his pipe either!

Slim jumped to another log and kept staring into the foaming water, but Nevers was nowhere to be seen.

The fellas on the dam stood silent as they watched. Ben felt as if he were suffocating.

"There!" Mac shouted, when Nevers's head popped up.

But at the same instant a stick of pine shot out of the sluice straight for him. Before anyone could yell a warning, Slim grabbed Nevers's collar and plucked him out of the water.

The fellas ran along the bank, and Jimmy reached out with a pike pole and guided Slim and Nevers's log to shore.

"Thank ye kindly, Jimmy," Slim said, his Stetson still in place and his gray eyes twinkling. "I didn't think to grab a pike pole before I jumped."

Jimmy helped Nevers off the log.

"You thought plenty fast!" Ben said.

"I'll say," Dick nodded slowly. "That boy was an inch from having his boots hung from a tree."

Nevers's voice trembled as he turned to Slim. "You saved my hide." Nevers swallowed and tried not to cry. "I swear, if you hadn't a been there to fish me out—"

"Weren't nothing," Slim said. Stepping onto shore, he took his pipe out of his mouth and checked the bowl. "But it looks like my pipe took on a little water." He tapped it on his knee, and everyone laughed, except Klondike who kept staring at the ground.

After all the logs had run through the chute, Mike came back to the wanigan. "You boys ready for your ride?"

Ben said, "Being that Nevers had that spill, I think we'd better walk."

"We're riding," Nevers said.

"I like your spunk!" Mike clapped Nevers's shoulder. "This boy's not even dried out, and he's up for a second sluice run."

Ben looked at Mike.

"What's on your mind?"

"I can't believe Klondike never made a move to help."

"I was outta reach," Nevers said.

"Outta reach! That coward left you to drown."

"Didn't surprise me none," Mike said.

"How can that be?"

"Have you heard how lumberjacks are either hiders or seekers?"

Ben nodded. "Pa told us that seekers head to the woods for adventure, while hiders are running from something."

"Would you guess that Klondike is a hider or a seeker?"

"That's easy," Nevers said. "Anybody who goes prospecting for gold up in Alaska is a seeker."

"You'd be right if that fella was telling the truth."

"Are you saying Klondike's a liar?" Ben frowned.

"His whole life is made up," Mike said.

"What about all those stories about sled dogs and gold nuggets?" Nevers asked.

"Not a word of it's true."

"But he's always talking about Chilkoot Pass and the Yukon."

"Klondike's never been near any of those places."

"Why don't you fellas call him out then?" Nevers said.

"These river pigs look tough on the outside, but most of 'em got soft hearts. We all know Klondike did a mean, low thing that he ain't facing up to."

"What sort of thing?" Ben asked.

"Let's just say he compromised a young lady's reputation and run off."

"And you're all helping him live a lie?"

"You could put it that way. But I figure every fella should be free to choose the life he wants to lead. What's fitting for one might not be right for the other. Plus you've heard what the good book says about judging others?"

"Judge not lest ye be judged?" Ben asked.

Mike nodded. "How can I look down on someone, when I've fallen short of the mark myself at times?"

"So all them stories was made up?" Nevers asked.

"Every one," Mike said.

Ben thought for a moment. "When you put everything together, it does makes sense."

"In what way?" Mike asked.

"I figure it's not much of a stretch for a coward to turn out to be a liar."

"Well I know one thing that's true," Mike said.

"What's that?" Ben asked.

"We need to get this scow moving if we want to set up camp before dark. You boys stow the loose utensils. Jimmy and Mac will be helping us with the piloting."

Before they pushed off, Mike untied the firewood raft so it could float through the dam on its own, and Dick portaged the canoe. Then Jimmy and Mac stood on the corners of the front deck, while Sard perched in the middle.

"Jimmy and Mac will help line us up."

"Where do you want us?" Ben asked.

"You'd better ride inside. You'll see plenty enough through the front door."

Before the dam came into view, Ben could hear the racing water. And when they swung out of the last bend, the wanigan was moving almost as fast as it had on Dead Man's Rapids.

Ben looked at Nevers. "Is it too late to walk?"

"I was thinking that same thing."

As they drew closer to the dam, Jimmy and Mac started calling, "a little right," or "a smidge left."

The chute looked way too narrow to Ben, but the wanigan went faster and faster.

Only twenty yards from the sluice, Mac yelled, "A touch right!"

Then Jimmy hollered, "Hold her there."

As the wanigan shot between the cribs, Ben and Nevers clutched the edge of the dishing-up table. The hull scraped on the right crib, and for a second, the whole boat shuddered. Ben's knuckles went white, as the front deck hung in empty air.

Then they plunged straight down.

"Ahhhh . . ." Nevers yelled. The dishes rattled in the cupboard, a logging chain slid across the floor and clunked into a flour barrel. And the hanging lantern swung wildly above their heads.

After a quick free fall, the wanigan hit the flat below the dam, and the front deck bucked up. The floor cracked, sounding as if it had split in half. At the same time the stovepipe jarred loose and fell behind the woodstove, kicking up a cloud of ash and soot. Ben and Nevers tumbled to the floor, and a cupboard door popped open, spilling tin plates and cups on top of them.

Then, as suddenly as the run had begun, it was over. The wanigan drifted into a pool, and the lantern stopped swinging.

"You okay?" Ben asked, peering through the ash cloud at Nevers.

"I reckon so," Nevers said. "When we hit that chute, your eyes was as big as two buckeyes in a barrel of buttermilk."

"I saw your fingernails digging into that tabletop."

"Just admit you were both scared witless," Mike laughed through the back door. "Your mama hummingbird's gonna need a refill of sugar water."

At the same time, Sard stepped inside and clapped his hands. "That's what I call a fine ride!"

But when Sard saw the dishes piled around Ben and Nevers, he said, "This ain't playtime, girls. Get your fannies off the floor, and clean up this mess. We got two miles of river ahead of us."

28

Of Toads and Tar Buckets

"I WISH it would warm up," Ben said, after seeing a light frost on the deck the next morning.

"You gone and done it again," Nevers said.

"Done what?"

"You wished after I warned you to watch yourself."

"Don't be silly," Ben said.

"I know what I seen so far on this trip."

"It's May, but it feels like March," Ben said. "We deserve a little sunshine."

"Let's hope a little is all we get."

When it was still cool the next day, Ben teased Nevers by fanning himself and saying, "I'm burning up in all this heat."

Nevers ignored Ben. And he didn't say anything the next morning when the breeze slackened, and it began to warm up.

When it was blazing hot by noon, Ben finally turned to Nevers and asked, "You think there might be something to my wishing?"

"Only a blind fella would reckon otherwise."

For the next week, it stayed hot and still. The sun beat down on the river all day, and the logs got so warm that pine pitch oozed out, leaving a shiny, rainbow film on the water. A turpentine smell filled the air. And sticky black goo coated the rocks along the shore.

The sun burned the faces of the men, especially Jimmy, who had pale, freckled skin like Ben. Despite the heat, Mike kept his wool stocking cap on, and his ears, protected by only a few strands of frizzy hair, blistered badly.

The hummingbird dish had to be filled every day, and Nevers said, "Sard's sugar bowl is like the Pied Piper's flute. We're collecting more birds as we go along."

To Ben's surprise, the heat even slowed down Mike's talking. One afternoon he started telling about a legendary treasure hidden on the Blackwater and marked by a sword stuck in a tree. But he lost his steam part way through the story and quit.

To add to their misery, clouds of newly hatched mosquitoes appeared. The fellas used bacon grease for bug dope, but the fat turned rancid and smelled nearly as bad as Sard's sausages.

One evening Ben and Nevers piled green leaves on the campfire to smoke away the bugs. But the smudge gave Nevers a coughing fit, and the mosquitoes weren't bothered at all.

The heat was the hardest to bear at night. As Ben climbed into bed, he said, "I can't understand it. In Minnesota it's always chilly in the spring."

"Well chilly it ain't," Nevers said. "I might as well be in Carolina. And sleeping by that cookstove makes it twice as hot."

Sard chuckled from the far corner. "Too bad one of you chuckleheads wasn't smart enough to pick this bed when you had the chance. I got a nice cool breeze up here."

Ben knew that Sard was exaggerating, but it would have been nice to be farther from the stove. Baking bread in the morning got the wanigan so hot that they were sweating before dawn. And cooking all day meant the stove never cooled down.

Along with the heat, the river tested the patience of the men, too. The current slowed the farther north they went, and the sharp bends made it easy for the logs to hang up.

"All the twists and turns are making me dizzy," Nevers said.

"And those logs are moving slower than a toad in a tar bucket." Mac looked more worried than usual. "The river's so crooked we're driving three miles to get one mile closer to Canada."

After supper, Mike pulled off his socks and stared at his pink, swollen feet. His stub of a little toe was bleeding. "My feet feel like they been parboiled."

"I got blisters on my blisters," Dick drawled.

"But the leeches don't mind the heat a bit," Jimmy said. Pulling a fat leech off his ankle, he tossed it into the campfire and watched it sizzle on the coals.

Mike propped his giant feet on a log in front of the fire. "Maybe I can smoke these dogs dry."

"Careful you don't cook your toes," Jimmy said.

"Old Sard might salt and pepper them," Dick nodded, talking even slower than he usually did.

The next morning when Dick reached into the lard bucket, he held up his hand and watched the warm fat drip off his fingers. "No sense larding up with this," he wiped his hand on his pants.

"I always figured that cold water would be harder on log drivers than warm," Ben said.

"You can dress for the cold," Jimmy said. "But there's no hiding from heat."

Mike nodded. "And the warm water softens up your feet so they blister real easy." Mike had been walking around camp barefoot to toughen up his skin.

That night as Ben and Nevers got ready for bed, the air was dead calm. The heat was stifling for Ben, who slept only inches from the tar-paper roof. And the stench of garlic sausage was getting stronger every day.

When a fat mosquito buzzed past Ben's face, he slapped it against his cheek and felt a splatter of blood.

Sard, who had taken to leaving his shirt off day and night, laughed in the dark, "Grow yourself some chin whiskers, Little Ben. It gives the skeeters less dining territory."

When Nevers smacked two more mosquitoes, Sard laughed again.

Nevers said, "It's too bad that some folks take pleasure from people suffering."

But Sard was already snoring.

The farther north they went, the more the current slowed. One morning after Dick dynamited a splash dam, he said, "I coulda spit in the river for all the water that blast added."

More sandbars and rocks appeared every day. And so many logs got hung up that all three crews ended up working side by side.

One afternoon Mike said, "In all my days I ain't never seen the Blackwater fall so fast."

"What happens if it keeps going down?" Ben asked.

"Let's hope it don't. One year we had to hike out and leave the logs until it rained later that fall. But some years it stays dry right into the winter."

"Then what?" Nevers asked.

"Then why don't you dunderheads stop asking so blamed many questions?" Sard hollered from the front.

Mike ignored Sard. "The next spring we start driving the logs from where we left off. That's if the company hasn't lost so much money it's gone bust."

"Then nobody gets paid?" Nevers asked.

"It happens. Every drive is a crapshoot. That's why there's a big push to build railroads. Trains ain't cheap, but they run rain or shine."

Later that night, as the boys were getting ready for bed, Ben asked, "Hear that?"

"I don't hear nothing."

"That's what's so strange. The logs are poking along so slow it's like the river's gone and died."

"Why don't you try wishing for rain?"

"Don't be silly. I could wish 'til I was blue in the face, and it wouldn't make a whit of difference."

"I seen enough to disagree."

"It's easy to make something out of nothing, but that don't mean it's sensible."

"You coulda wished twice for all the words you wasted."

"Anything to shut you up. Here goes." Ben tilted his head back, closed his eyes, and spoke so fast that the words ran together: "I wish it would rain."

Ben grinned. "You happy now?"

"Can't you see this is serious business?"

"Okay, how about this?" Lifting his head, Ben spoke slow and deep like a minister: "I seriously wish it would rain."

"That's a sorry excuse for a joke."

29

If Wishes Were Horses

BEN WOKE feeling like he'd spent the night in a sauna. Back home when the house got too hot, he slept on the back porch. A tall maple shaded that side of the house, and once the sun went down, a breeze usually blew up from the river. But the wanigan had been deathly still and hot.

It remained strangely quiet when the boys stepped outside to wash up. "Suppose the birds aren't singing 'cause they're nesting?" Ben asked.

"Maybe their voices just dried up in the heat?"

"Speaking of the heat," Ben looked up at the clear sky and teased Nevers. "I see my wish for rain is working real well."

Nevers ignored him, but Ben went on. "You ever hear that old nursery rhyme about horses?"

"You mean the one about twenty white horses on a hill?" Nevers asked.

"No, the one that goes, 'If wishes were horses, then beggars would ride.'"

"Cut it out," Nevers said.

Later that morning, when Jimmy stepped into the kitchen to dish up, he began with his usual, "'Tis a fine day—." But when he felt the blast of heat from the cookstove and saw the sweat running down Nevers's face, even he couldn't think of anything positive to say.

The heat wave continued for two more days. The sun beat down, and the logs kept oozing sap in the sluggish current.

Mike told Dick, "We're turning back and forth so much, I'm afraid I'm going to meet my own self coming back." Mike had finally taken off his bucket-sized stocking hat, and his frizzy hair was sticking up every which way.

"Your own self would give anyone a scare with that wild mop of hair," Dick grinned, showing his black gums.

Along with the heat some near-invisible bugs called no-see-ums emerged. They were so pesky that Mike said, "These is the meanest, flesh-hungry critters I ever laid eyes on."

Ben nodded, trying to dig one out of the hair behind his left ear. "They got knives for teeth."

"Too bad we can't dynamite the danged bugs," Dick said.

"Don't get any ideas," Mac said.

"These bugs ain't nothing compared to what we had up in Alaska," Klondike said, but everyone ignored him.

That afternoon Nevers got excited and pointed to some dark clouds in the north. "It's already raining off yonder."

"It can't rain without—" But before Ben could get out the word *wind*, a breeze skittered across the water. And a moment later thunder rumbled in the distance.

"What I tell you?" Nevers said.

"That sky's got an ornery yellow tinge," Mike said.

Within the hour gusts were kicking up waves on the river. The crowns of the pines whipped from side to side, and the leaves on the birch trees turned upside down.

Mac called everyone back to camp early, like a general drawing up a battle plan. While he talked to the fellas, the wind blew so hard that they had to lean to keep their balance. But there was still no rain.

After Mac finished with the men, he turned to Ben. "I know you just pitched the tents, but you'd better break 'em down."

Just then a jagged flash of lightning crackled across the sky, followed by a long peal of thunder. Mac hollered to Dick, "Get some fellas to pull the bateau up on shore and lash the canoe down." Then he told Sard, "Better douse the fire in your stove in case we have to shelter inside."

By the time the boys had the tents stowed, everyone had crowded into the wanigan.

Ben was looking out the front door when the first wave of rain raced up the river, turning the water to brown froth.

"It's like a moving waterfall!" Nevers said.

"Close the door!" Mac hollered.

Just as Ben slid the door shut, the rain swept over the deck and hit the wanigan. The roof sounded like a pail of marbles had been dumped out of the sky.

"We'd better close this too," Mac said, sliding the back door partly shut. Ben could barely hear Mac over the wind and the rain.

Nevers's hands shook as he struck a match to light the overhead lantern. The wind buffeted the wanigan so hard that the lantern creaked as it swung from side to side. If the wanigan broke apart and sank, would they have to walk all the way to Canada?

With the fellas crowded elbow to elbow, the stink of wet wool, sweat, and stale tobacco was getting stronger by the minute. And for the first time that Ben could recall, even Mike was quiet. These fellas lived with danger every day of their lives, yet the force of the storm had left them speechless.

Jimmy finally smiled at Ben, "Lucky you took down those tents, otherwise you'd be fetching 'em from the next county."

That got the fellas talking about other storms. Jimmy told about a nor'easter that hit Bangor, Maine, when he was a boy. Mike mentioned a squall that he'd sailed through on Lake

Superior, and Mac recalled a tornado from his boyhood in Racine, Wisconsin.

When the wind suddenly dropped off, Nevers said, "Maybe that was the worst of it?" but before anyone had a chance to agree, an even stronger gust kicked up.

"Whoa," Sard said, as the stovepipe whistled. "If she blows any harder, it'll suck the stove lids up the chimney."

Ben heard a tree crash in the woods and then another. He looked through the door and watched a tall spruce sway. As the wind blew harder, the spruce leaned more. And each time that it tilted it came back less.

"There she goes," Nevers said, as the spruce finally tipped all the way to the ground.

"I thought big trees fell fast?" Ben said.

"If the ground is soft, sometimes the roots just pull out gradual like that," Jimmy said.

Just then Ben felt the floor shake as the strongest gust yet hit the wanigan. No one moved or spoke. Over the screeching of the wind, Ben heard the sharp crack of more trees snapping off.

"By the sound of that," Mike said, "I'd say some of them trees ain't falling so slow and gentle."

"Lordy, Lordy," Nevers whispered, his eyes huge in the lamplight. "I never woulda guessed how powerful a wish could be."

30

Dead and Downed

"*AUFWACHEN*, you river pigs! Wake up!"

Sard slid the door open, and Ben squinted in the sunlight.

"I can't be cooking breakfast with you clowns snoozing on my floor," Sard said.

The men groaned and swore. They were sprawled out right where they'd dozed off last night. And everyone but Jimmy looked like they could use a few hours more sleep.

Ignoring the cussing, Sard clanked a pot down on the stove. "I got to start a fire to simmer the beans."

"Now you're talking," Jimmy said. "It's daylight in the swamp, boys. Let's clear out the kitchen."

With the men still grumbling, Ben and Nevers stepped outside. The air felt wet and heavy. Thick clouds of mosquitoes hummed. And the birds on the shore looked confused, flitting from one branch to another and tweeting loudly. One glance at the tangle of fallen trees told Ben that the crew was fortunate to be alive.

Nevers whistled. "Those pines snapped off like twigs."

Ben nodded. "We're lucky they didn't smash the wanigan."

Ben saw that other trees had ripped out soggy root balls of earth and rock as they went down. The pine smell in the air reminded him of a sawmill.

143

"Morning, boys."

Ben was surprised to see Mike step out of the woods. "It is bad?" Ben asked, swishing at the hundreds of mosquitoes that hummed around his head.

"I scouted a good ways north. Windfalls are laying every which way."

Just then the mother hummingbird zipped past Ben's ear and let out a sharp chirp.

Ben looked over at the nest. The two babies stretched out their necks and beat their wings, jostling each other and begging for food. "I can't believe they made it through the storm."

Mike smiled. "If their mama hadn't wrapped that nest in spider silk, they woulda busted it open long ago."

The mother hummingbird buzzed over Ben again. Then she circled the rain-filled dish of water on the deck railing.

"You gonna gawk all day, dunderheads!" Sard hollered through the door. "Pretend you're useful, and fill that bird's dish."

When Ben headed inside to warm a pan of sugar water, Nevers said, "I reckon you musta learned your lesson."

"Don't start in on that wishing again."

"You'd be right foolish not to watch yourself."

"I made that silly wish four days ago."

"I saw what I saw, and I'll believe what I choose to."

Nevers was so convinced that Ben had brought on the storm that he watched him all morning to make sure he didn't wish anything accidentally. If Ben so much as used a word that began with the letter *w*, Nevers hollered, "Hold her right there!"

It got so bad that Ben finally said, "I wi—"

"Stop right there," Nevers said.

"I was only gonna say"—Ben talked so fast that Nevers couldn't cut him off—"that I wish you'd stop worrying about what I'm gonna say next."

"Suit yourself," Nevers said. "But don't blame me if you bring a calamity down on us all."

Clearing the river of windfalls left the men with mud up to their ears. Through the day Ben heard several dynamite blasts, which normally would have left Dick smiling, but he only said, "I never et so much mud."

"She's a mess," Slim nodded. Even he had muck spattered over his pants. "But at least the water's rising."

After two days of channel clearing, the logs were finally bumping along at normal speed. Jimmy cocked his head and smiled. "That rumbling means our cork pine's finally riding high again."

Ben was amazed at how fast the sluggish, mud-bound river had surged back to life. And the spirits of the crew soared with the rising water.

Over the next three days the wanigan passed through some of the wildest and prettiest country Ben had ever seen.

"It's like a moving picture show," Nevers said, as he breathed in the rich scent of the plum and chokecherry blossoms.

"Picture yourself with this, sawdust brain," Sard said, handing Nevers a knife to peel the potatoes.

As spectacular as the wilderness was, it reminded Ben of how far he'd come from home. He found himself lonesome for little things like the click of Evy's knitting needles and the warm smell of her chocolate cake. He longed to hear the piano music that drifted down to the boardinghouse at night. And he even missed Pa chiding him about forgetting his chores.

Late in the afternoon they floated past a grove of giant cedars. The shaggy, gray-barked trees were so tall that only dappled silver light reached the carpet of moss and ferns below.

"Smell that?" Ben asked, as they stood on the back deck and breathed in the heady scent of damp cedar.

"It's dark and earthy but sweet," Nevers said.

"The only thing I smell is laziness," Sard yelled.

The next day the land got higher, and they passed a stand of massive white pine. "Those must be two hundred feet tall," Nevers said.

"Two hundred is a stretch," Mike said. "A few might push one hundred fifty."

Just then the wanigan rounded a bend, and the pine were gone. In their place stumps and brush piles extended as far as Ben could see.

"A clearcut?" Nevers asked.

"But why so many scorched stumps?" Ben asked.

"There musta been a forest fire," Nevers said.

"How come only the stumps near the bank are charred?"

"You've got a good eye," Mike said. "Only a few are burnt for a reason. Don't suppose you've heard of the Dead and Downed Timber Act?"

Ben and Nevers shook their heads.

"Most folks haven't. It gives loggers the right to harvest fire-damaged timber on Indian reservations. Sounds sensible to not let trees go to waste, don't it?"

Ben nodded.

"But one look at this cut shows what it's come to. If a company wants to log on Indian land, they start a brush fire and scorch a few trees. They might as well splash black paint on the bark for the harm it does. Then they report the whole stand as fire damaged."

"How can they get away with it?" Ben asked.

"They slip cash to the right people. I figure they logged two million board feet here."

"That's stealing," Nevers said.

"It wouldn't be the first time a politician wrote a law that dressed up stealing to make his friends rich," Mike said.

"And my guess is it won't be the last," Ben said.

31

The Widow Johnson

WHEN MIKE RETURNED to the wanigan for the final move of the day, he said, "We should reach Johnson's Crossing before dark. It'll be the last chance to restock before our final push."

"Johnson's Crossing sounds like a real town," Nevers said.

"Only a dozen families live there, but lots of folks pass through," Mike said. "Able Johnson and his wife started a store at the Crossing about five years back. Able passed on last spring, and his widow's been running it on her own."

Just then the mother hummingbird buzzed over Mike's head and landed on her nest. The babies pushed against each other, chirping and reaching up to get fed.

"It won't be long before they're flying," Ben smiled.

"Unless they knock each other into the river first," Mike said.

When they neared Johnson's Crossing, Ben and Nevers walked to the front for a better view.

Ben pointed to the rickety log bridge that spanned the river. "I'll bet it's called the Crossing 'cause of that bridge."

"You're getting more brilliant every day, professor," Sard shook his head.

Unlike Esko's Emporium, there weren't any signs in front of the store, and no one was waiting to greet them except Mac.

After the boys tied up the wanigan, they followed Mac, Sard, and Mike up the bank. The neatly kept store was built out of rounded logs, and it had a wide front porch. A second story with two curtained windows faced the river.

As they reached the front steps, Mike said, "Wait 'til you meet Anna Johnson. She's a real spunky gal."

Sard walked through the door, calling, "Anybody home?"

Ben was surprised at how neat the store looked. Hardware and tools were shelved on one side, with food and housewares on the other. A case under the counter displayed ammunition, knives, scissors, and sewing items.

Sard leaned on the counter. "I said, anybody here?"

"Of course there's somebody here." Anna Johnson stepped from behind a curtain and looked at Sard. "You suppose this store can run itself?"

Anna was broad shouldered and half a head taller than Sard. Her blonde hair was tied back with a white kerchief, and she wore a blue-checked cotton dress that matched the color of her pretty, blue eyes.

"You don't have to get sassy," Sard said.

"Ask a question that shows you have a brain, and you'll get less sass," Anna said.

Mike chuckled. "I told you she was feisty! Hey there, Anna."

"Good to see you, Hungry Mike," Anna said, shaking his hand. Ben was surprised to see the muscles in her forearm stand out.

"You still got a good grip," Mike smiled. "You know Mac, and this here is Sard, our new cook, and his cookees."

Anna looked at Sard and frowned. "Sard's a strange name if I ever heard one."

"My full name is Sardman, Peter Sardman."

"So you're *Deutsch*?"

"*Ja.*"

"I was married to a Swede, but I'm German, too. From Wiesbaden. My maiden name was Anna Wiebusch." She looked more closely at Sard. "You're the cook, eh?"

"*Ja*," Sard said.

Anna turned to Mike, "I can't believe you let him cook in that filthy apron!" Then she scolded Ben and Nevers: "You boys ought to pitch him in the river once in a while and wash him off."

Ben figured Sard would get mad, but he laughed instead and said something in German, which made her laugh even more.

Anna and Sard kept jabbering in German, ignoring everyone else. Since the only German words Ben had learned from Sard were *dummkopf* and *mischbrot*, he had no idea what they were talking about. Mac and Mike got bored and walked outside.

Sard finally placed his order and counted some money onto the counter. Then he switched back to English and told the boys which supplies to carry down to the wanigan.

Ben was disappointed when he saw the first thing they had to carry. "Not another sack of rye!"

Sard grinned. "Anna appreciates black bread, too."

Nevers shook his head. "Imagine the odds of the only two storekeepers on this river favoring rye flour!"

"Instead of wishing for rain I shoulda wished for a store that sold white flour," Ben said, as he and Nevers shouldered the heavy sack and wobbled out the door.

Sard stayed behind and chatted with Anna.

When they got to the wanigan, Nevers said, "I can't get over how that widow lady chewed Sard out. But he never even got mad."

"When it comes to Sard, nothing surprises me anymore."

Mike said, "I'm gonna check on my crew. If Sard keeps chewing the fat, you boys might be cooking on your own tonight."

The whole time Ben and Nevers set up camp, they heard Sard and Anna up in the store talking German and laughing.

When Sard finally came down the hill, he was smiling.

"So what did you talk about so long?" Ben asked.

"We mainly visited about back home. Anna grew up not far from me. Imagine that!"

"She seems like a nice lady," Nevers said.

Sard looked back toward the store for a moment. Then he said, "That's enough gabbing, Snicklefritz. We gotta get the swill ready for our pigs."

32

The Sound of Silence

THE NEXT MORNING Ben woke up with an odd feeling. At first he thought it was the brightness. Now that it was June the sun rose so early that there was a hint of pink in the sky by four o'clock. But something else felt strange. "You asleep?" Ben whispered.

"I been awake awhile," Nevers said.

"Me, too." The air was warm and still. Ben lifted his head and looked outside. He suddenly knew what was wrong. Sard wasn't singing. Ben glanced into the corner. "Sard's bunk is empty."

"He must be washing up," Nevers said.

"Why isn't he singing then?"

Ben and Nevers stepped onto the back deck. A light fog had settled over the water, and the men were quiet in the tents.

"You don't suppose?" Ben looked toward the store. The upstairs windows were open, and the curtains were swaying ever so gently. "Is that snoring I hear?"

"If that don't beat all!" Nevers and Ben kept staring at the windows, not wanting to believe what they could plainly see was true.

After the boys washed up, Nevers asked, "Suppose we should start breakfast?"

"What do you say we give the fellas a break from all that boiled food?" Ben said.

"We got fresh eggs from Mrs. Johnson. We can fry up a mess of eggs and bacon and taters."

"And how about a stack of sweat pads to finish things off?"

"And let's make 'em with white flour," Nevers smiled.

Since Ben and Nevers hadn't made pancakes for a while, they got the batter too thick, but once they thinned it out, they managed to fry up a passable stack of sweat pads.

When Mike tromped across the gangplank for breakfast, he stopped so fast that Jimmy bumped into him. "Am I dreaming, or do I smell pancakes?" Mike stepped inside and grinned. "It's a miracle I tell you! Angels have landed on earth and rescued us all!"

The crew was so excited to see the pancakes that they were all dished up and eating before Slim asked, "Where's Sard?"

Ben and Nevers shrugged. Everyone was silent for a minute. Then Mike said, "Why that old sausage boiler! I can't believe it!"

Ben and Nevers both smiled.

"Believe what?" Dick said. "Make sense."

"Sard has gone and got himself a girlfriend."

"You're daft," Jimmy said. "There ain't a woman between here and Boothbay that would put up with—" He stopped when he saw Mike nodding toward the store. Jimmy's eyes widened. "Not that pretty widow lady? And Sard!"

Mike kept nodding and smiling.

"I done lost all faith in womankind," Dick said.

"Me too," Mac said.

The whole time the fellas ate they kept peering toward the store and shaking their heads.

It wasn't long before a German song floated down from the upstairs window. And this time two voices were singing, and one of them wasn't half-bad.

"It's true, by golly," Dick stared at the store window and blinked like he was having a hard time convincing himself. "And I thought I'd seen everything."

Ben was pouring Slim his second cup of blackjack, when Sard walked down the hill from the store. Ben was so shocked by Sard's looks that he sloshed some coffee on Slim's boot.

"Steady there," Slim said.

"You're not gonna believe this," Ben nodded.

Slim and Jimmy turned.

"Would you look at that old rapscallion?" Jimmy whispered.

"What's that?" Dick asked. Then he turned too.

Pretty soon all the fellas were gawking like they were witnessing the second coming. Mike kept shaking his head like he'd gone swimming and got water stuck in his ears.

Sard had on a brand-new gray shirt and denim pants. And as he got closer, Ben could see that his boots and his leather eye patch had been polished up.

Nobody spoke until Sard stopped and said, "I see that the boys have served you a nice breakfast."

"And what did Peter Sardman have for breakfast?" Jimmy asked with a sly grin.

"You old sausage boiler!" Mike said. "Tell us what you did to earn them fancy new pants."

"Who woulda guessed that Old Sard was an expert at entertaining lonesome widow ladies?" Dick grinned.

Sard took the ribbing with a smile. When the laughter settled down, he turned to Mac. "Mrs. Johnson has asked me to help her run the store. So if it's all right with you, I'll be staying on here."

As the meaning of Sard's words sank in, Ben looked at

Nevers. Nevers's face showed the same confusion that Ben felt. Was it time to celebrate? Or should they be scared because they might soon be cooking on their own?

"The drive'll be done in a couple weeks," Sard continued. "So Little Ben and Snicklefritz should be able to handle the cooking."

"That's why you're dressed like a storekeeper?" Jimmy asked.

Sard nodded. "As we speak, Mrs. Johnson is burning my other clothes. And she's asked me to cut back on my cooking."

Everybody laughed again. Then Mike stood up and raised his coffee cup. "Good-bye and good riddance to Sard's greasy apron."

"Hear, hear," the others chanted and lifted their cups.

The only fella who didn't join the toast was Mac, who mumbled, "First a heat wave, then a storm, now a German cook playing Romeo. What's next?"

33

Alles Hat Ein Ende

SARD WALKED DOWN to the wanigan with Ben and Nevers. "Sorry to leave you boys in the lurch like this. I bet you never thought you'd lose two cooks on the same drive."

"You said you'd rather muck out a stable than be a store-keeper," Ben said.

"And that you had no patience for women," Nevers added.

"So I did. But I've decided it'd be a sin not to stay on here."

"What's working in a store got to do with sinning?" Nevers asked.

"I'm talking about Mrs. Johnson. To my mind, leaving a pretty widow lady like her all alone is about the biggest sin a fella could commit."

Ben shook his head at Sard's upside-down thinking.

Sard walked to his bunk and dragged out his gunnysack.

"You want a cup of water to take your pills?" Nevers asked.

"I feel so good I'm skipping my dosing for today."

Before Sard left, he grinned and said, "You dunderheads take care. And if you fry some doughnuts, don't go burning the boat up."

Sard started up the bank, but he turned one last time and called, *"Alles hat ein Ende, nur die Wurst hat zwei."*

"What's that supposed to mean?" Ben asked.

"It's an old German proverb: 'Everything has an end. Only the sausage has two.' Ha, ha, ha," he laughed all the way to the store.

Ben turned to Nevers. "I still can't figure out why a lady like Mrs. Johnson would want to spend time with Sard."

"Just 'cause that widow lady's pretty doesn't mean she's got good eyesight," Nevers smiled.

"And if she wants to get close to Sard, her nose better not work so good either."

The next morning Ben woke to the scent of wild raspberry blossoms drifting through the doorway. Though it was still dark outside, he heard Nevers stirring below.

As Ben got up and lit the lantern, Nevers said, "I never thought I'd say it, but it's hard staying asleep with all this peace and quiet."

"Are you saying that you miss Sard's singing?"

"I wouldn't go that far."

"Since we're up, we might as well start breakfast."

"It's gonna be so much fun cooking without Sard around."

"And we should have time to make those doughnuts."

Ben and Nevers had just finished forming the *mischbrot* dough into loaves, when they heard someone on the deck.

"It's right early for anybody to be up," Nevers said.

"Maybe Sard's ghost has come to haunt us?"

"It's only me," Jimmy called through the door. "I'm so used to Sard croaking out his songs, it was too peaceful to sleep."

"Us too," Ben said.

Jimmy said, "It's like when I was a boy, and my daddy moved us into a house next to a train track. At first none of us got a wink of sleep with the freights clattering by. But after a week, we never even heard those trains."

"If you're comparing Sard's singing to trains, a train wreck might be closer to home," Nevers smiled.

"True," Jimmy nodded. "You want me to get some stove wood?"

"You don't have to do that," Ben said.

"I might as well. There's no way I'm going back to sleep. Unless one of you boys wants to croon me a German lullaby."

The boys visited with Jimmy and took their time getting the bread in the oven and starting the beans.

"Ain't it sweet to not have Sard yelling at us?" Ben smiled.

"I'm as happy as a hog in an acorn patch," Nevers said.

Ben was feeling relaxed until he checked his pocket watch. "Batching up that bread took longer than I figured. We're running a bit late."

"How late?"

"If we skip the doughnuts, we might be okay."

Nevers hurried and grabbed a pot. "If you slice the bacon, I'll start the oatmeal and open a can of prunes."

"I'd better get the coffee water boiling first," Ben said, as he ran to the stove and chunked in two sticks of wood. Suddenly sweating, he filled the coffeepot and grabbed the slab of bacon.

"We're lucky Jimmy filled the wood box for us," Nevers said.

Ben nodded, slicing the bacon as quickly as he could.

By the time they'd set the food on the dishing-up table, the fellows were already standing on the back deck.

"Everything okay in here?" Mac poked his head in.

"Ouch!" Ben yelped. He was reaching into the oven to take out the last of the bread, and Mac had startled him.

"You burn yourself?"

"No," Ben lied. Not only was Ben burnt, but his heart was pounding, and he was soaked with sweat from hustling around the steaming-hot kitchen. "I feel like I've run ten miles," he whispered to Nevers.

"I'm plumb tuckered out, too."

Just then Mike spoke through the door. "Looks like Sard ain't the only one who's flown the coop on you cookees."

"What do you mean?" Ben asked.

"Take a gander out here," Mike said.

Ben lifted his apron to wipe the sweat from his forehead and stepped outside. Mike pointed toward the empty hummingbird nest.

"The birds were there last night," Ben said.

"Well they're gone today," Mike said.

"Maybe those birds decided to stay on at the Crossing and keep Old Sard company," Jimmy said.

Dick piped up farther back. "I figure Sard's got enough to keep his hands full."

The fellas all laughed.

After everyone had finished their breakfast, Ben looked at the stack of dirty plates and crusted pots. "Don't that seem like a bigger pile of dirty dishes than normal?"

Nevers was about to answer, when Jimmy stopped by.

"Hey, Jimmy," Nevers said, "The nose bags ain't quite ready yet." What he didn't tell Jimmy was that he hadn't even started slicing the bread, which was still too hot for sandwich making.

"I figured that," Jimmy said. "Me and Dick was just talking. Is there any chance you boys know how to make white bread?"

Ben and Nevers both smiled.

"Last winter we cooked white bread every day," Nevers said.

"And we got Pa's recipe memorized," Ben said.

"That's music to my ears," Jimmy said.

"We'll bake some first thing tomorrow," Ben said.

"I'll be looking forward to it."

When the crews were finally on their way, Ben took a deep breath for the first time all morning. "Whew!" he said, sitting on a flour barrel.

"For a while there we was jumping like a pair a long-tailed cats in a room full of rocking chairs," Nevers said.

"That's a good one," Ben laughed. "Running this kitchen

might be more work than we bargained for, but at least nobody's calling us dummkopfs every time we turn around."

"I was starting to think dunderhead was my middle name."

"I still can't believe we got rid of Sard," Ben said.

"Maybe the folks in Canada heard he was coming, and they commissioned Mrs. Johnson to derail him?"

Ben grinned. "We'd better decide what we're making for the first lunch. Mike and his crew'll be back before we know it."

"Let's bake some biscuits to go along with the beans."

"Mike would like that."

"Do we have enough blackjack?"

Ben checked the coffeepot. "It's almost empty."

"And we're low on water," Nevers said.

"We'll have to bake the biscuits when we get back."

The boys were ready to climb into the canoe, when Ben glanced down and said, "Look what we're forgetting."

"Our calks!" Nevers grinned.

"We'd never hear the end of it if we sank our canoe."

The boys paddled to a stream and filled the water cans in record time. But when they turned the canoe to head back, Ben decided to play a trick. "What's floating over there?" He pointed.

"Where?" Nevers looked downstream.

"No. Behind you," Ben said. "It's a dead man!"

"A dead man!" Nevers yelled. Twisting around in his seat, he shifted his weight so fast that both water cans tipped over.

As soon as Ben saw Nevers's face, he was sorry for teasing him, but it was too late to take it back. And it was too late to stop both of them from spilling into the river.

Ben stood as quickly as he could in the waist-deep water and said, "I was only joshing."

But Nevers was already stumbling toward shore.

Ben hollered, "I said I was joking."

Nevers stopped and turned. "What did you say?"

"I was only joking."

"You mean there's no body?" Nevers stared at him, panting.

"There's no body," Ben shook his head.

"That was dirt mean!" Nevers splashed Ben and spewed out a yard-long string of cuss words.

"I'm sorry, but I thought it'd be funny."

"Well it weren't." Nevers was still breathing hard.

Ben apologized again, as they dumped the water out of the canoe and refilled the water cans, but Nevers wouldn't look at him.

The boys paddled as fast as they could, but by the time they got back to the wanigan, Mike's crew had already helped themselves to some leftover bread and beans.

Mike was waiting to greet them. "You boys look a bit soggy. Didn't I warn you that a canoe can wet you just like a baby?"

Ben was about to explain what had happened when he realized that anything he said would only give Mike more ammunition for teasing. So he just said, "Sorry."

When it was time to move the wanigan, Mike asked, "Should I get someone to steer, or do you two want to take the bow?"

"What do you say?" Ben turned to Nevers.

"Let's give her a try," Nevers said.

"This stretch of river's pretty tame," Mike said. "It'll be good practice."

Instead of leaving, Mike kept looking around the kitchen.

"You need something?" Nevers asked.

"Nope. But I do have a question."

"What is it?" Ben asked.

"Well, seeing as you have a couple barrels of Gold Medal flour over there, I was thinking—"

"Jimmy already asked if we'd bake white bread," Nevers said.

"Really?" Mike grinned.

"We plan on serving some tomorrow," Ben said.

"Hallelujah. Let's get this scow moving."

Nevers took the first turn steering, and Ben said, "I'm real sorry I played such a mean trick on you."

When Nevers didn't say anything, Ben continued, "I just wasn't thinking at the time."

Nevers finally said, "I know you meant to be funny. But like I told you, I got bad memories. Sorry I cussed you out like that."

"You had every right," Ben said.

Nevers looked downriver. "It might sound strange to say it, but the whole time we're on the water, I keep waiting for Sard to start singing."

"Me too. Do you think it'll work out with him and the widow?"

"Mrs. Johnson's already got him in new clothes. I reckon a shave and a bath will come next. By fall she'll have him looking as spiffy as an undertaker."

A short while later, Mike called, "Curve coming."

Ben looked downriver. He and Nevers had been talking so much that they hadn't noticed the bend.

"Take her more inside," Mike spoke louder this time.

Since the curve was a long way off, Ben couldn't see any hurry, but Mike said, "Start turning! The bow swings slow."

Ben helped Nevers pull on the oar, but the wanigan kept drifting toward the bank.

"We shoulda studied Sard's steering closer," Ben said, noticing some birch trees hanging over the bank.

"Keep pulling!" Mike yelled.

"We are!" Ben said, leaning on the oar with all his might.

"It's gonna be close," Nevers said.

Suddenly the wanigan bumped over a rock, nearly jarring the oar out of their hands. And at the same time a birch top hit the bow. As the branches crackled and flexed, Ben yelled, "Duck!"

The tree snapped over the railing and smacked into the front wall with a crack. The whole boat shuddered as the branches dragged across the roof and banged into the stovepipe.

When it was over, Mike asked, "You okay up there?"

"I think so," Ben said, staring at the birch leaves and broken twigs that littered the deck.

Mike stepped up front to survey the damage. "We're lucky you didn't run us aground."

"I guess we're not such good steerers," Nevers said.

"At least you dummkopfs don't sing up here," Mike chuckled. "You'd better get this mess swept up before the fellas—"

"What's going on here?" a voice asked.

Ben turned. Jimmy was standing onshore beside Mac and grinning. "By that pile of greenery onboard I'd say you boys must be taking up leaf collecting."

But Mac wasn't smiling as he glared at Ben and Nevers. "Don't you know that boats ain't made to be drove through the woods?"

"I just hope they don't plan on cooking us birch-leaf soup tonight," Jimmy grinned.

Later, Slim started off dinner by looking at Mac and asking, "Is it true what I heard? That two boys on this river just got their pilot's licenses revoked today?"

34

Stewed Prunes and Pickle Pie

THE NEXT MORNING Ben was hoping that breakfast would go smoother. But by the time they had the white bread in the oven and the beans cooking, they were running behind.

"We'll have to skip those doughnuts again," Nevers said.

"I really wanted to try Pa's recipe without the spuds."

"Maybe tomorrow," Nevers said. "I'll slice the bacon."

"And I'll heat the prunes. Though one thing we don't need no more of right now is heat." Hurrying to grab a pan, Ben wiped his forehead with the back of his hand.

"She's gonna be another lard melter," Nevers said.

"I almost wish—"

"Don't start that wishing again," Nevers said.

"I was just gonna say I almost wish Sard was here helping."

"I know what you mean. He rode us hard, but he was right quick in the kitchen."

"Well we sure ain't paddling back to the Crossing and rescuing him from the widow lady," Ben laughed.

The white bread turned out a little heavy—Ben wondered if the starter was getting weak—but no one complained.

"Just like old times," Dick said, giving the boys their first compliment, as he sopped up his bean juice with a slice of bread.

"Now that you got Jack's bread recipe down pat," Mike said, "do suppose you could take a crack at a vinegar pie?"

Jimmy grinned. "You know when Mike asks for one pie he means an even dozen!"

"I don't think we're up to pie making just yet," Ben said. He could tell that Nevers was ready to overrule him, but he winked to keep him quiet.

Later Ben said, "I thought a pie would be more fun as a surprise."

"Good idea," Nevers said.

The next day they worked on the pies between the first and second lunch. Recalling Pa's recipe as best they could, they rolled the crust, and pressed it into a half-dozen pie tins. But when Ben lifted a tin to hide it in the cupboard, he frowned.

"What's wrong?" Nevers asked.

"The crust feels heftier than I remember."

"It'll lighten up when it bakes," Nevers said.

When they started to mix the pie filling, Ben said, "I think Pa used three parts hot water to one part vinegar."

But Nevers said, "It's a vinegar pie, not a water pie."

They compromised on equal parts of vinegar and water and slipped the pies into the oven after the second lunch.

That evening after the men finished their meal, Ben and Nevers carried the pies up to the campfire.

"What's this?" Mike grinned so wide his ears lifted out of his frizzy hair. "After all these pieless miles, are my eyes deceiving me?"

"It's vinegar pie," Nevers said.

"And I thought I was gonna have to wait 'til the border to get a taste of pie!"

"Here you go." Ben cut a wedge and slid it onto Mike's plate, while the rest of the fellas crowded in to get their share.

Mike took a big bite, and Ben watched to see his reaction. When Mike ate, he often closed his eyes and went, "Um, um, um," but as he chewed on the vinegar pie, his eyes got bigger and his lips puckered.

Mike finally swallowed and took a swig of coffee.

"Too much vinegar?" Ben asked.

"It's a touch sour." Mike set down his cup and studied the piece left on his plate. "In fact, I think you boys ought to change the name to pickle pie."

Ben looked at Nevers. "I told you we overdid it."

The rest of the fellas were wondering if they dared try a piece. But Jimmy, who had already stirred a bite of pie into his bean juice, downed it with a big smile. "She's a little tart, and that crust takes some serious jaw work. But to my mind, there ain't no such thing as bad pie."

"You're right there," Dick nodded, digging in. "Like Old Sard woulda said, pie is pie. I thank you boys for your effort."

After the third day of baking white bread, Mike came down to the wanigan after supper, looking uneasy.

"What's on your mind?" Ben asked.

"You know that white bread you been making?"

Ben nodded.

"It's fine bread. A mirror image of your pa's. Light and fluffy."

"That's good."

"As odd as I feel saying it—" Mike paused and rubbed his whiskers. "Well, I'll lay her on the line. The fellas have been talking, and we miss the crunchy taste of that black bread."

"You want Sard's *mischbrot* back!" Nevers asked.

"No, no. We wouldn't want you to switch altogether, but it might be nice to change over once in a while."

"How about if we make rye bread one day and white the next?" Ben asked.

"Or maybe two days of rye and one of white? However you boys decide to mix it up is fine with us."

After Mike left, Nevers said, "Can you believe it? After all that complaining about black bread being as heavy as a boat anchor, now they want it back?"

"To tell the truth, I got used to that dark bread myself."

"I have to admit I miss it some, too," Nevers said. "It's like biting into something real."

35

The Wiener War

THE FOLLOWING EVENING Ben and Nevers served a supper of biscuits and gravy and beans. The biscuits won high praise.

When the men were sitting back and sipping their blackjack, Dick said, "You know, the thing I liked most about this meal wasn't the biscuits."

"Was it that wicked good gravy?" Jimmy asked.

"Nope," Dick smiled, "My favorite thing was not having any god-awful sausage."

"I'll drink to that," Mike said, and the fellas raised their devil cups in a toast.

"I was tasting that garlic in my sleep," Dick said.

"What do you say we rid ourselves of the last of those stink-eroos?" Mike stood up.

"Right now?" Jimmy asked.

"No time like the present," Dick said.

"There's only a dozen sausages left," Nevers said.

"That settles it." Dick led the way down to the wanigan.

When Dick unhooked the first sausage from the ceiling, he said, "It's all slimy."

"Sard used to scrape the mold off," Ben said.

"That dirty hash slinger," Dick said. "All the more reason to dump 'em."

"You ready, fellas?" Jimmy asked, positioning himself in the doorway, while Mike stood on the back deck.

"Let's put this garbage where it belongs." Dick sang out, tossing a sausage to Jimmy who threw it to Mike, who pitched it into the river.

The rest of the crew, who had gathered on the bank, cheered at the first splash.

"One down!" Jimmy hollered.

Ben and Nevers watched the three fellas work like a bucket brigade, tossing one sausage after another into the river, and hooting with laughter the whole time.

Jimmy suddenly said, "Wait just a minute there."

"The wieners are as old as the sausages," Dick said.

Ben couldn't understand what was going on until he looked inside and saw Jimmy and Dick tugging back and forth, fighting over a wiener.

"I don't see no mold on these," Jimmy hollered.

"They're rotten. I say we toss 'em!"

"But I like wieners with my beans," Jimmy yelled, as they kept tussling.

One of the men on the bank stepped closer to see what was going on, and he called, "They're battling over a wiener." And everyone laughed.

When Dick saw that Jimmy wouldn't give in, he said, "Have it your way. At least the wieners ain't so garlicky."

"By the way," Mike said, "Jimmy's right about wieners going good with beans."

Since Pa kept his recipes in his head, Ben and Nevers's cooking included a good amount of guessing. Some of the meals didn't turn out great, but the fellas only teased them a little. One morning when the biscuits came out flat, Dick looked at one sideways and said, "Is this a biscuit or a cracker?"

Everyone appreciated the change in menu except Jimmy. He got nervous whenever anything looked different, saying, "Fancy is fine as long as you don't tinker with that bean recipe."

The boys had been cooking a whole week before they finally found time to make doughnuts. Though they scorched the first panful, they got the temperature under control and didn't start any fires.

Jimmy kindly said, "That smoky flavor ain't bad at all."

For desserts they baked everything but molasses cookies, which had been Sard's staple. Their first try at a cake came out heavy, but no one complained. And when their oatmeal cookies were lumpy, Mac only said, "A little extra chewing keeps the fellas occupied so they don't have time to complain."

Mike was even forgiving one evening when they served an overly sweet lemon pie. He dug in with a smile, saying, "This might taste like a piece of Christmas candy, but it beats your pickle pie hands down."

The night they had the lemon pie, Ben and Nevers set aside two pieces for themselves, which they ate after they fed the men. "Pa told me that my ma was partial to lemon pie. He said she liked the meringue piled so high." Ben held his hand two inches above the plate.

"Well, I don't think we're up to trying anything as fancy as meringue. My mama favored sweet potato pie."

"I never had it, but it sounds good," Ben said.

Picking up two forks, he handed one to Nevers. "If only my ma had lived long enough to sit down and share a piece a pie with me. I'd give anything to see her face one more time and to hear her laugh. Pa said her laugh was real joyful."

Nevers nodded. "She musta been a fine lady."

After a moment of silence, Ben held up a bite of lemon pie on his fork and said, "To fine ladies and sweet pie."

Nevers smiled and lifted a bite of his own, "Amen."

Of all the meals that Ben and Nevers cooked, the fellas' favorite came courtesy of Dynamite Dick, who sent back another stringer of fish with Mike early one afternoon.

When Mike came back to the wanigan later that day, he asked, "Have you got those fish filleted? The fellas are looking forward to a fish fry."

"We chopped 'em up already," Nevers said.

"Chopped?"

"Yep," Ben nodded at a big kettle on the stove. "Nevers and I decided we'd make Sard's fish stew again."

"You mean that Finlander soup with the heads and all?" Mike's shoulders slumped.

Ben tried not to grin as Mike walked over and lifted the lid. "Hey!" he hollered. "This is empty!"

That night the fellas praised the fried fish and taters as their best meal yet. And when Jimmy lined up for seconds, he paid the ultimate compliment, saying, "This fish is so good I didn't even take seconds on the beans."

"Should we skip the beans next time?" Nevers asked.

"Hold your horses right there," Jimmy said, turning to give Nevers a talking-to, but he stopped when he saw Nevers's smile. "You had me going for a second."

Mike grinned. "Taking Jimmy's beans away would be like separating Dick from his dynamite."

After the big push of water from the storm, dry weather returned, and the water level began dropping again.

Ben asked Mike, "What if the logs get stuck again?"

"We've got plenty of water to make the border now. All the homesteads we've been passing are a good sign that Thompson Rapids is getting close. And do you remember why a falling river is good?"

"It keeps the logs centered?"

"You've been paying attention. Other than one pebbly rapids

ahead, we should be on easy street." When Mike saw that Nevers was listening, he added, "Why, if things go as good as I think they will, we may be able to take it easy and have three lunches every day."

"Three lunches!" Nevers said. "As it is Ben and I can't hardly sit down to eat a bite ourselves!"

Mike winked at Ben. "And two breakfasts would be nice."

"You said there wasn't no such a thing as two break—" Nevers stopped when he saw Mike's grin. "That ain't even funny."

36

The Last Rapids

"I CAN'T BELIEVE we've got only one rapids to go," Nevers stared back upriver.

"Seems like we were breaking ice just yesterday." Ben nodded. "And look how thick and green all the leaves are."

"That's how log drives always are," Mike said, biting into the last of the five doughnuts he'd stuck on his fingers. "You start off in the snow and cold. But before you know it, summer's in full bloom, and the logs are floating in the millpond."

"Is Boulder Rapids an easy one?" Ben asked.

"The upper part's gentle enough," Mike said, "but the lower section has got a few nuggets in it."

"I hope we don't wreck the wanigan after making it all this way," Nevers said.

"That ain't likely," Mike said. "But the wood butchers have got to bust up the boat anyway."

"Why would they bust it up?" Nevers asked.

Ben said, "We can't float back upstream, and there's no railroad, so they have to take it apart and haul it by wagon."

Mike finished his doughnut and took a swig of coffee. "They can't salvage everything on a boat this old, but they'll save what they can. The ribs in front are the hardest to replace, and they always try to reuse those."

"You fellas gonna sit around all afternoon chawing on doughnuts, or are you ready to move this wanigan?"

Ben turned and saw that Jimmy was back. Ben was glad that Jimmy had agreed to handle the bow when they shot Boulder Rapids.

"Bout time you got here, you old bean eater," Mike grinned.

After they'd cast off the lines and pulled in the gangplanks, Ben grinned at Nevers. "Ain't it nice to not have to worry about steering for a change?"

"And even better, our cooking days are done for this trip."

"You boys plan on hitting the saloons when we get to town?" Jimmy teased.

Nevers shook his head. "What I'm hankering for is a good bath." He looked at his sap-blackened palms. "Now that we're done messing with those sticky balsam, I'm scrubbing these clean."

"Is that why I noticed a pine flavor to all your cooking?" Jimmy laughed.

A short while later Mike called, "Listen up."

A duck flew low over the wanigan, quacking as its wings whistled. And in the distance Ben heard the logs bumping together. He tilted his head and concentrated. "Rapids ahead."

"She's right around the next bend," Jimmy nodded.

Only a few minutes later Ben was surprised to see big waves popping up at the head of the rapids. "Mike said there were only a few small nuggets here."

"It's called Boulder Rapids for good reason," Jimmy said. "We just head straight down the gut and hope."

"Ready up there?" Mike called.

"She's on a good line," Jimmy said. Then he turned to Ben and Nevers. "I'd rather be riding a log than steering this old scow. I like being closer to the water."

Jimmy dipped his oar. Then he looked at Ben. "You'd

better grab something solid. We'll be dragging bottom shortly."

Ben moved to the doorway, but he didn't bother to brace himself, because he couldn't see any sudden drops ahead.

Suddenly the front of the wanigan jumped up, knocking Ben to his knees.

"I told you to hold on," Jimmy laughed.

Nevers had been smart and grabbed the door frame.

Ben felt the floor flex under him, as they scraped over a big boulder. Then the boat bumped over a second and a third rock, going faster and faster the whole time.

Ben was gripping the doorway when they dragged across the biggest boulder of all. Jimmy lurched forward, nearly losing his hold on the oar.

"Hang on!" Jimmy yelled. The floor heaved up with a loud crack. The wanigan shuddered and almost stopped. Ben waited anxiously as the hull teetered from side to side.

"If we get stuck, do we have to swim to shore?" Nevers asked.

But just then, the boat tilted downstream and slid free.

"Whew!" Jimmy breathed. "We made her! For a minute I thought Dick was gonna have to blast us loose."

"He woulda liked that," Nevers said.

"But Dick wouldna left much for the wood butchers to take apart," Jimmy smiled.

37

A Pair of Flashing Eyes

"Is that Canada over yonder?" Nevers pointed across the Rainy River as they tied the wanigan to some trees below the town of Thompson Rapids.

"You're looking at her," Mike said. "If you feel like paddling, you can canoe all the way to Hudson Bay from here."

"I reckon I've come far enough north. Did they name this place after a fella called Thompson?" Nevers asked.

"I bet he was a rich lumberman," Ben said.

"Nope," Mike said. "David Thompson was an explorer and a fur trader. Folks say he mapped four million square miles all the way to the Pacific."

Nevers whistled. "He must have been a traveling fool."

"He covered more territory than any of us river pigs ever will."

Ben looked up at the town of Thompson Rapids. Built on a low hillside overlooking the Rainy River, it was about the size of Blackwater but had a lot fewer saloons. The streets were dusty, but the board sidewalks looked brand new.

"I thought it'd be lots bigger," Ben said.

"The sawmill is the only real business here," Mike said. "If you want to see a boomtown, Koochiching is just downriver. A fella named Backus is building a big dam and paper mill there."

"Look," Nevers pointed toward the pond in front of the saw-mill. "They're already sorting our logs."

"They have to check the stamp marks and boom our logs together," Mike said.

"What's booming?" Nevers asked.

"See how they're chaining the logs end to end and making a big circle?" Mike pointed. "The scalers measure each log and tally the board feet before it goes into the mill. But we don't have to worry about that. Once the logs hit the Rainy River, our contract was complete."

Just then a cheer went up from the sorting pond. Ben saw that a crowd had gathered down the shore.

"Must be a log-rolling contest," Ben said.

"I'll bet Slim dunked somebody," Mike said. "Every jack in the north woods wants to take on Slim."

Ben and Nevers followed a dirt path along the river until they got to the sorting pond. Two fellas were standing on each end of a floating log and eyeing each other. When Ben got closer, he said, "It's Dick. The other fella must be a local."

"Looks like the whole town's turned out," Nevers said.

Ben and Nevers scooted to the front of the crowd as a man on one side raised a pistol into the air.

"Hey, Mayor," a fella called to the man with the gun.

"Ready!" the mayor called. When Dick and the other man nodded, the mayor fired a shot.

Everybody cheered as the men's calk boots dug into bark, and the log began to spin. The smoke from the revolver drifted toward Nevers and made him cough. "Look at 'em go!" Nevers said, as the log kicked water into the air.

The crowd groaned only a few minutes later when Dick dug in his spikes and stopped the log so fast that the other fella pitched into the river. But the folks all cheered when the next man dunked Klondike in ten seconds flat.

After each contest, two men stationed on the bank reached

out with pike poles and pulled the log into shore. The winner stepped onto dry land, while the loser had to wade in.

Some of the matches took thirty seconds; others went on for ten or fifteen minutes. But as more fellas were eliminated, it was clear that the last battle was going to be between Slim and a fella from Thompson Rapids named Burt. Burt was a whole lot bigger than Slim, and he looked strong.

Slim quieted the crowd every time he took down one of the locals. "I don't know how he stays so calm," Nevers said.

"Slim is always steady and cool," Ben said.

The other birlers waved their arms and hollered as they fought to keep their balance. But no matter how fast Slim's boots moved, his upper body stayed still, and his steel-gray eyes stayed focused. With his hands slightly out, his weathered Stetson on his head, and his pipe set in the corner of his mouth, Slim's lightning-quick calks dumped one fella after another.

When Slim and Burt finally faced off, the crowd got quiet. Even the fellas who were placing bets hushed their voices. But once the mayor's pistol went off, everyone cheered.

Slim and Burt started slowly, testing each other by spinning the log one way and the other. Then Burt made the first move. He ran in place, whirling the log so fast that it kicked up rooster tails of water. Then, without breaking stride, he stomped down hard. His calks stopped the log cold, and his weight drove it way under, nearly tipping Slim.

But Slim turned in a blink and spun the log the opposite way.

Then Burt countered by digging in his calks so quickly that Slim almost lost his pipe.

As the battle waged, Slim looked tired. "Burt's too big and strong," Nevers whispered.

Ben had his fingers crossed, but he was worried, too.

Slim's shoulders sagged, and he looked tippy. But just when Ben was ready to give up hope, Slim tried a new trick.

It started when Burt made another jump, planning to come

down hard and pitch Slim off. But Slim surprised Burt by jumping at the same time. And instead of going straight up, Slim leaped out toward the end of the log. He went so high that everyone in the crowd held their breath. It reminded Ben of the time Slim leaped off the dam to save Nevers.

Slim was still airborne when Burt came down, and the log dipped so low that water sloshed over Burt's boots. For the first time, Burt was off balance. He waved his arms and bellowed, "Whoa!" Then, just when he looked ready to catch himself, Slim landed on his end of the log and gave it a quick turn.

The look in Burt's eyes told everyone he was done. He flailed his arms and let out a half-hearted yell. But he'd passed his tipping point.

When Burt hit the water, the crowd went silent. Then their eyes shifted to Slim.

True to his nature, Slim didn't boast. He only tipped his Stetson politely. Suddenly everyone clapped and cheered. And the crowd kept clapping as the fellas pulled the log in, and Slim stepped onto the bank.

Once Slim was on shore, he extended his hand to Burt and helped him climb out of the water. Burt shook Slim's hand and said, "Fine birling," which brought on a final round of applause.

Shortly after the Blackwater crew congratulated Slim, Mac passed out the pay slips. "That's perfect timing, Mac," Dick said. He was so excited that he was almost talking at a normal speed. "The Itasca steamboat should be leaving within the hour. Koochiching here we come!"

Dick and the other fellas hustled down to the wanigan and grabbed the flour sacks, or turkeys, that they used to carry their possessions. When Dick opened his sack and pulled out a pair of shiny black oxfords, Nevers asked, "Why'd you lug those fancy shoes all this way?"

"I bring my town shoes on every drive." Dick said, lacing up his oxfords. "Respectable ladies don't like to dance with a fella in spiked boots."

"When was the last time a respectable lady danced with you?" Slim asked, and everyone chuckled.

"Why don't you just celebrate here?" Ben asked.

"There's too many churches," Dick said.

"I only see two," Ben said.

"That's two too many for me," Dick grinned, spitting through his missing tooth. "And once I tire out all the gals in Koochiching, I'm gonna double my fun by heading across the river to Fort Frances, Canada."

When Nevers saw that Jimmy was standing empty-handed, he asked, "Aren't you going with the other fellas?"

"To tell the truth, I'm a little lonesome for home."

"You rascal," Mac said. "You really are sweet on that new wife of yours."

"She's mighty pretty," Jimmy smiled. "And I promised her a Fourth of July picnic."

Mike hung back while the other fellas walked up to the steamboat dock. Then he turned to Ben and Nevers and said, "I want to thank you boys for doing your best on this trip. I know it was a struggle working with that old sausage boiler, Sard, but you both grew into man-sized cooks. If you ever have the urge to hire on another drive, you can sling hash for me any day."

"And I appreciate you teaching me the proper way to tie up a wanigan," Ben grinned.

"All this talking is making me hungry," Mike said. "Before that steamboat leaves, I know a little restaurant where I can get me a doubleheader."

After the paddle wheeler left for Koochiching, Ben and Nevers walked back to the wanigan. Mac was giving directions to two men who'd unloaded a pile of tools from a wagon.

After the workmen left, Ben asked, "The wood butchers?"

Mac nodded. "They'll be taking the wanigan apart tomorrow."

"Our bunks and all?" Nevers asked.

"They're tearing her down to the last plank," Mac said. "After I settle up at the bank in the morning, I can give you boys a wagon ride back to Blackwater."

"We'd appreciate that," Ben said.

"By the way. One of those carpenters gave me a report on your pa."

"Is he okay?" Ben asked.

"You can put your mind at ease. That fella said the day after we left, he saw Charlie and your pa fishing together. And later that week he stopped by Wilson's Boardinghouse, and your pa and Evy were baking a chocolate cake together."

"No fooling?"

"That doesn't surprise me," Mac said. "Your pa has a short fuse, but he cools down fast."

"Ben's wish came true," Nevers smiled.

"Since we're not leaving 'til morning," Mac said, "you boys have the rest of the day to explore the town. You ain't about to get liquored up, are you?"

Ben laughed. "We'll keep our noses clean."

The first thing Ben noticed about Main Street was how new everything looked. The biggest stores in Thompson Rapids were a general mercantile and a fancy-looking place called Carlson's Clothier. There was also a butcher shop, a barbershop, a few smaller stores, and a bank, unlike Blackwater, where the saloon keepers did the banking. Farther up the hill stood several rows of clapboard houses and the two churches.

"With only one saloon in town I can see why the fellas headed downriver," Ben said.

"Some towns in Carolina got five or six churches and not a single saloon," Nevers said.

"No fooling?" Ben said.

"There's some dry counties in my neck of the woods where you can't buy a drop of legal liquor nowhere."

"They'd never get lumberjacks to work there," Ben said.

"Now there's a sight for sore eyes," Nevers pointed.

Halfway down the block a young girl sat at a table in front of the mercantile store. A signboard propped beside her read, "Church Social Tickets, 10 Cents."

Ben saw that the girl had soft, black curls and that a white bonnet framed her face.

"She sure looks pretty," Nevers whispered.

"I think I'm in love!" Ben said.

Nevers started to walk faster, and so did Ben.

Suddenly Nevers jumped off the sidewalk and began to run down the street.

"Hey," Ben shouted. "No fair!"

Nevers only laughed.

Sprinting after Nevers, Ben pulled even in a few strides. But Nevers jammed an elbow in Ben's ribs. Laughing, Ben elbowed him back. They kept running hard and pushing at each other.

Ben was close enough to the girl to see that her skin was incredibly white compared to the sunburned faces of the river pigs. Then it happened.

Nevers nudged Ben toward the sidewalk, and the tip of his calk boot caught on a board. Ben watched the girl's bright-blue eyes flash open in horror as he stumbled forward and fell.

When Ben went down, his other boot tripped Nevers, who fell, too. Still laughing and tangled up like a pair of wrestling bear cubs, the boys hit the dirt and rolled over, their calk boots kicking up dust and their arms flailing.

When his somersault was done, Ben opened his eyes and found himself lying in the street, looking up at the pretty girl. She'd jumped out of her chair and clapped her hand over her mouth to keep from screaming.

Nevers's legs had pinned Ben down.

"Get off," Ben tried to stop laughing and catch his breath.

As Ben sat up, Nevers pointed to the back of Ben's wrist, which was bleeding. "My calks must have cut you," he said. Then noticing that his own shirtsleeve was torn, Nevers ripped off a strip of wool and handed it to Ben for a bandage.

"Thanks," Ben said, grinning as he wrapped his wrist and stood up.

The girl had taken her hand off her mouth, but she was staring like she'd just watched a tornado blow by.

Ben looked at the church social sign and shrugged his shoulders. "We'd buy a ticket, but we'll be long gone by Sunday."

"Maybe next year," Nevers said.

"Sure," Ben said, still chuckling as the boys turned and headed back to the wanigan. "Maybe next year."

Afterword

IMAGINE A thirty-below-zero morning in northern Minnesota during the winter of 1899. Pretend for a moment that you are a lumberjack looking up at a white pine tree 180 feet tall and so broad that you and your partner can't encircle it with your arms. Now consider the challenge of felling such a giant tree, using only an axe and a two-man crosscut saw, cutting it into sixteen-foot lengths, loading the logs onto a sled pulled by a four-horse team, and hauling them five miles on an ice road to the nearest frozen riverbank.

By the end of the winter, the eighty lumberjacks working in your camp will have hauled seven million board feet of logs and piled them beside the river. That would be a major accomplishment, but now consider that your job is only half done. Once the giant logs are staged beside the river, they still have to be delivered to a market. Without any railroads nearby, your only choice is to start a spring log drive and float all that timber one hundred miles to a sawmill on the Canadian border.

The tradition of log drives in America dates back to early colonial history. In seventeenth-century New England surveyors hired by the British navy reserved the tallest and straightest white pine for the Crown. After the trees were felled and limbed, men drove them downriver to the Atlantic coast, where they were milled into ships' masts and planking.

As the timber industry expanded through the 1700s and 1800s, log drives remained the most efficient method for delivering wood to lumber mills. Each spring, from the Penobscot and Kennebec Rivers in Maine to the Columbia and Willamette Rivers in Oregon, rugged men known as river pigs or river rats guided the logs downriver. Legendary for their strength and toughness, these log drivers endured freezing-cold water, sixteen-hour days, and life-threatening logjams. Clothed all in wool, the men coated their legs and feet with lard each morning to protect their skin from the icy waters. They wore calk boots equipped with sharp metal spikes that helped them balance on the floating logs, but they still faced the ever-present danger of falling between the logs and getting crushed or swept away by the rushing current.

Many log drives covered more than one hundred miles, and in the case of the Connecticut River logs were driven more than three hundred miles from the New Hampshire–Quebec border to mills in Massachusetts. The river pigs were paid well—an average of two dollars per day, twice the rate that lumberjacks got during the winter logging season. The harsh conditions merited the extra money; it was often said that every river driver was qualified to work as a lumberjack, but not every jack was tough enough to work as a river pig.

Once spring arrived, most lumber companies contracted with a log-driving company to deliver their logs. The drive company relied on labor agents, known as man catchers, to hire the river pigs for the drive. A foreman, who was often called a walking boss, supervised three separate crews of men.

The jam crew was an elite group who worked ahead of the drive, clearing the river of obstacles such as boulders, deadheads, and fallen trees. Their goal was to break up small logjams before they became serious.

The drive crew stayed with the main body of logs and worked to keep them moving. These men were experts at handling peaveys and pike poles and were famous for their ability to balance on logs as they floated downstream. They enjoyed showing off their skill as birlers, or log rollers. After the drive reached its final destination, log-rolling contests often determined the champion for that season.

The sacking crew, or rear crew, was left with the most miserable job of all. They trailed behind the drive and freed logs that got hung up on the bank, lost in sloughs, or grounded. They spent a good portion of their day wading in ice-cold water and slogging through mud.

In addition to the river pigs, the driving company also hired cooks, who traveled on a wanigan, or floating cookshack, which supplied meals for the men. The wanigan was a flat-bottomed boat, twenty to thirty feet long, equipped with bunks, a wood range, and a full kitchen. The wanigan also carried the tools that the river pigs needed.

The men ate four meals each day: breakfast, first lunch, second lunch, and dinner. Breakfast and dinner were dished up in the wanigan and eaten outside, but the men had to carry their lunches in "nose bags" made of canvas and equipped with shoulder straps. Some drives had a second bunk wanigan for the men to sleep in, but if the drive had only a single wanigan, the cooks slept inside while the rest of the crew camped in tents or lean-tos on the riverbank.

The wanigan also towed a large double-bowed rowboat called a bateau, which was used to carry men up and down the river. The wanigan was stocked with staples at the beginning of the trip, and it was resupplied along the way by purchasing food at country stores or directly from farmers. In remote locations the foreman often had to arrange for supplies to be delivered.

The jam crew did their best to prevent logjams. But if one did form, it could back up millions of feet of timber and flood the land for miles, putting the drive and the men's lives in jeopardy. If a jam stayed in place too long, the river could flow around the sides, dropping the water level so fast that the logs were left "high and dry."

Dynamite was a last resort to break up jams, as it damaged too much valuable timber. The first attempt usually fell to the most experienced man in the jam crew, who at great risk to his personal safety walked into the riverbed to determine which logs needed to be pried out of the way. He had a rope tied around his waist, and the men waiting on the bank were ready to pull him to safety if the jam broke loose. Even with such precautions, it wasn't uncommon for the volunteer to be swept away by a wall of logs and water.

The largest logjam in history happened in 1894 on the Mississippi River near Little Falls, Minnesota. Logs piled up to an astonishing mass that was a half mile wide, seven miles long, and sixty feet thick. Estimates put the total amount of timber at four billion board feet. It took 150 lumberjacks, five teams of horses, and one steam engine working for six months to get the logs moving again.

Along with the constant dangers and hardships of driving logs, the biggest problem companies faced was the unpredictable water levels. Both too much and too little water presented challenges. High water caused by spring floods or sudden storms often floated the logs over the riverbanks and left them stranded in forests and fields. Getting the logs back into the stream took back-breaking work from the sacking crew. Each log was marked with a "stamp hammer" symbol or a bark mark that was registered with the state surveyor general to identify the company who owned it, but "pirates" sometimes attempted to steal the timber. Logs that couldn't be retrieved (along with logs that became waterlogged and sank) caused an average loss of about 10 percent on each drive.

The biggest threat to the success of log drives was drought.

Low water caused by a lack of winter snow cover or inadequate spring rains could make it difficult or impossible to complete the drive. Companies built dams to help regulate the flow of the rivers, yet it wasn't uncommon for low water to stall an entire drive. During dry summers, drives were often suspended in the hope that fall rains would raise the water enough to get the logs moving. But if the drought lasted too long, the logs could remain stranded until the following year. Extended dry periods made it difficult for the drive companies to make their payroll and in the worst cases brought financial ruin. A dry winter followed by a lack of spring rain in 1900–1901 made drive conditions so difficult that nearly all of the logs harvested that season remained stranded in the woods, leaving sawmills idle.

Unpredictable weather, along with the environmental damage caused by logs scouring streambeds, provided an incentive for logging companies to turn to steam locomotives for transporting logs. Though it took a major investment to build and to maintain railroads in the remote locations where the largest stands of pine typically grew, in most cases it was cost effective and greatly improved the efficiency and safety of timber production. But as the twentieth century progressed and more highways were built in the north woods, trucks gradually began to displace logging railroads as the preferred method of transportation. Since roads were cheaper to build and maintain than railroads, and trucks were more versatile in accessing steep slopes and isolated areas, the trend toward trucking continued until the last of the classic logging railroads were eliminated in the 1960s.

Long after the proliferation of highways, log drives remained popular on some of America's most famous rivers. Crews drove the Little Fork River in Minnesota as late as 1937, and the Clearwater River in Idaho until 1971. The last log drive in America took place on the Kennebec River in Maine during the summer of 1976.

Educational Resources

Books

Blackwater Ben by William Durbin (University of Minnesota Press, 2014)

Daylight in the Swamp by Robert W. Wells (World's Work Limited, 1984)

Early Loggers in Minnesota by J. C. Ryan, volumes 1–5 (Minnesota Timber Producers Association, 1973–1986)

Tall Timber: A Pictorial History of Logging in the Upper Midwest by Tom Bacig and Fred Thompson (Voyageur Press, 1982)

Timber! by Ben Rajala (North Star Press, 1991)

The White Pine Industry in Minnesota by Agnes M. Larson (University of Minnesota Press, 2007)

Organizations

Cradle of Forestry in America, Portland, Oregon.
http://cradleofforestry.com/

Forest History Center, Grand Rapids, Minnesota.
http://sites.mnhs.org/historic-sites/forest-history-center

Forest History Society, Durham, North Carolina.
http://www.foresthistory.org/

Minnesota Historical Society, St. Paul, Minnesota.
http://www.mnhs.org/

World Forestry Center, Portland, Oregon.
http://www.worldforestry.org/

Acknowledgments

SPECIAL THANKS to Jeffrey Johns, Becky Jennings, Ed Nelson, and the staff of the Forest History Center in Grand Rapids, Minnesota; John Latimer, phenology expert and friend of KAXE Radio; Vic Zgaynor, otherwise known as Whitewater Slim; Skip Drake, northern district program manager for the Minnesota Historical Society; the Forest History Society; and the Minnesota Discovery Center in Chisholm, Minnesota.

William Durbin is a writer and former teacher who lives on Lake Vermilion at the edge of Minnesota's Boundary Waters wilderness. A winner of the Great Lakes Book Award and a two-time winner of the Minnesota Book Award, he has published eleven novels for young readers, including *The Broken Blade, Wintering, Song of Sampo Lake* (Minnesota, 2011), *The Darkest Evening* (Minnesota, 2011), and *Blackwater Ben* (Minnesota, 2014).

Barbara Durbin is a lifelong educator who has dedicated her career to inspiring students to be active readers, writers, and thinkers. She has been an elementary school teacher and has worked with gifted and talented programs.